Black Eden Publications Presents...

WITHDRAWN

Counterfeit

Dreams 4

A Coke White Dream

www.SashaRavae.com

BLACK EDEN PUBLICATIONS™

Counterfeit *Dreams* 4

ISBN: 978-1511836081

10 9 8 7 6 5 4 3 2 1

Printed in the United States

Counterfeit

Dreams 4

A Coke White Dream

Chapter 1

"How you holding up, bruh?" Sacario asked noticing Jewel's lifeless expression.

"I'm straight. Listen, Sacario, I know that before Golden passed the M.A.C. Boys to me, he was looking at you for who was gonna be up next. He made a mistake by choosing me. I want you to take over the M.A.C. Boys. I'm done with this shit, blood."

"Jewel, what are you talking about? I know that this is hard for you right now. It's hard for everyone, but don't you think that's a little drastic? What's the M.A.C. Boys without you?"

"Since I stepped up, mothafuckas have been dying all around me, and the people who I held closest are all gone. I wanted to believe that I was meant for this shit because Golden and Brandon spoke that life into me, but they were wrong. I did what Golden wanted me to do, and it worked at first, but to be responsible for the lives of my niggas, I failed ya'll. How can I live with the fact that Pop's dead because of me?"

"If that's the case then we're all responsible, Jewel. I hate to put it like this, but it was the young g's time. We all got one. Hating yourself isn't gonna bring him back."

"I kept Pop on this path, and it cost him his life. I have two sons to take care of now. I can't let them be raised into this shit. It has to be different for them. It has to be."

"So that's it?"

Jewel stared into the mirror and couldn't believe how far he'd come. It had been a year since Pop died, but he could still see him so vividly. Giving up his rights to the M.A.C. Boys was the hardest decision he ever had to make, and although the life still created a hidden spark in him, he had no choice but to change for the better. He had Reagan, Chase, and Jailen to think about.

"You ready, son?" Joe asked sitting down in a dark mahogany leather chair beside him.

"Ready as I'll ever be," he said continuing to tie his tie, "With all the money I put into this thing, I really don't have any other choice."

"Welcome to my world," Joe said laughing, "but I know it'll be worth it. Reagan loves you, and you love her. Some things in life are just that simple. It's about time ya'll do this."

"You're right."

Knock. Knock. Knock.

"It's open," Jewel yelled.

"Ay, nigga," K-2 said busting into the room, "You ready to walk that plank or what?" He couldn't help but laugh.

"I don't know why you laughing. I heard you about to be next," Jewel winked.

"The hell I am," he started to say, "Oh, hey, Joe, I didn't even see you sitting there."

"I bet you didn't," he said slowly standing up.

"I was just joking. You know, giving Jewel a hard time."

"Well, I don't play when it comes to my daughter and future granddaughter, Keith."

"Neither do I, sir," he hurried to say.

After Pop's funeral, K-2 decided to move back to the Bay, but this time with Gabrielle right by his side. With high school and her first year of college out of the way, she felt like she was ready to take on the world, but he wanted nothing more than to provide for her. As hard as it was, he decided to follow in Jewel's footsteps and put the M.A.C. Boys behind him too. He did have a baby on the way after all.

"Let me get out of here before I knock this boy out. I think we're about to start here pretty soon. Jewel, let's get a move on."

"I got this, Pops. Thank you though," he said beginning to get irritated.

"I'm just trying to help."

"I know," Jewel said taking a breath, "I'm sorry. My nerves are bad."

"Well, just try to relax," he said walking out of the room as Sacario walked in.

"How you doing, Mr. Sanchez, sir?"

"Good, Sacario, how bout yourself?"

"Can't complain."

"Glad to hear it," Joe said going to rejoin his wife Isabella before the ceremony began.

"I got exactly what you need," K-2 said shutting the door before he pulled out a bag of weed from his pants' pocket.

"In the tux though, blood?" Sacario asked laughing.

"You said that like it's a bad thing." He grabbed a small magazine that the church had laying around and broke down the green buds as Jewel continued to get dressed.

"What's up with you though?" Sacario asked walking up to Jewel, "I feel like I never see you anymore. Nigga, you didn't even let me throw you a bachelor party."

"I've been doing the family thang, bruh."

"It looks like it's working out. I'm proud of you, blood."

"Man, that nigga's bored," K-2 interrupted, "You out here bout to get married and got two kids. All your life consists of now is baby throw up and sports practices."

"Welcome to your future," Jewel mocked.

"'Not I,' said the cat," he said sealing the swisher he held in his hand, "I gotta keep it P.I. at all times."

"Here you go. Can't you just let this nigga be happy?"

"I'm just saying, I know you miss the life, blood."

"I do, but I gotta family to think about now. I mean we all have families, so we gotta do better, feel me?"

"How you lecturing him, and you never step foot outside the shop?" Sacario asked.

K-2 had always been quick with the cuts. All through high school, his potnahs never had to go to the barber shop because he would hook them up in his garage, but after wanting to follow behind Sacario into the M.A.C. Boys' elites, he put his talents aside and chose another path. It was definitely a dream come true when he was inducted into the organization. He looked up to Jewel and Sacario and valued their leadership, but after Pop's death, K-2 could see the change in Jewel, and it scared him. Jewel had climbed his way to the top, and in the blink of an eye, he let it all go. K-2 went back and forth with himself about going legit and separating from the clique, but when Gabrielle confirmed that she was pregnant, he decided that his time, unfortunately, had come too. He took the money he had been saving over the years and invested in himself, and soon thereafter, Rich City Cutz was born. Sacario wanted to be his silent partner, but for K-2, it was something he had to do on his own.

"We not talking about me," he said lighting the blunt.

"How's business though?" Jewel asked proud of his young homie's new venture.

"Popping as usual. Gabby be helping me with a lot of the administrative stuff, but I told her that I was gonna eventually have to hire somebody once she gets bigger."

"What she say?" he asked taking the blunt out of K-2's hand already knowing his little sister's reaction.

"That it's good as long as it's not another female," he said laughing.

"Speaking of females, what's been up with Diamond? She looked stressed out there when I saw her."

"Man, that's a whole 'nother story," he said shaking his head. He didn't even know where to start. "Enough about me. What's been up with you?"

"You know I got it rocking out in the Bay. I thought the transition was gon' set us back some, but so far, things have been smooth. We still miss you though. Niggas swear up and down you coming back."

"You not bout to Jay-Z niggas, are you?"

"Naw," Jewel said flattered, "I'm good where I'm at. After losing Brandon, Golden, and Pop, it's not the same no more. It doesn't even feel right, you know?"

"What doesn't feel right?" Diamond asked busting into the room. The mango and white-colored bouquet she held in her hand glittered in the sunlight that peered through the floor length windows.

"We'll be in the sanctuary, blood," K-2 said ashing the blunt before quickly putting it behind his ear.

"Yeah, hit me if you need anything. I'ma make sure that Kiko and Arianna are okay out there."

"Take your time," Jewel said finally relaxing a bit.

"The ceremony starts in like twenty minutes," Diamond said with her hand on her hip, "and you're not even all the way dressed yet."

"D, I got this," he said as K-2 and Sacario walked out of the room hoping to avoid their usual drama.

"Well, let me help you," she said grabbing his shirt and pulling him toward her.

"Where's Reagan?"

"Finishing up with her makeup," she said tracing her fingers across his chest.

"Maybe you should go check on her then," he said pulling away.

"Why would I do that when I can be here?"

"Diamond, come on, blood," he said feeling himself becoming tense again.

After Pop's funeral, Jewel decided that life was too short. He and Diamond had both been to hell and back, and he was ready to start over. As much as he loved being with his son every day, he could tell that he missed his mom, so he didn't stand in the way of Diamond regaining joint custody. They managed to work out a system, but with this newfound co-parent relationship, she was around more and more, and Reagan gravitated to her. With the birth of her son Chase, she was ready to put the past behind them. She had no more room in her heart to hold grudges, and soon, her hatred for Brandon dissipated with every smile her son made or every step he took, so when it came to her and Diamond coming together as mothers, she thought it was only right.

"Jewel, are you really gonna do this?"

"Why wouldn't I?" he asked staring into the mirror as he slipped his cream-colored suit jacket over his crisp white shirt.

"Because we have a child together, and I know you still have feelings for me."

"Diamond," he said turning around to face her, "Me and you have had this conversation more than once, and I'm mad that you chose my mothafucking wedding day to have it again."

"What do you expect me to say? I'm sorry I can't just turn my feelings off. I love you," she said wrapping her arms around his waist.

"Don't you feel just a little bad?"

"Bad about what?"

"That you're Reagan's maid of honor."

"No, not really. She took what was mine, and now, I want it back," she said lightly kissing his lips, "I'm done with the games, Jewel."

He pushed Diamond off of him fed up with her unwanted efforts. His heart belonged to Reagan, always had and always would, but she refused to accept it. Her love for Jewel and hate for Reagan made everything she did a little easier. She was determined to get her family back.

"Bye, Diamond, you're hella outta pocket. I try to keep shit cool with you for the sake of our son, but at this point, I feel like your priority is to fuck up my family," he said wiping his mouth, "Why are you even here?"

"I am your family. We're bound for life, so that's why I'm here."

"Tell that to my wife."

"Not wifey just yet, hunny," she laughed as she walked towards the door, "And believe me she knows. What's that saying? Keep your friends close and your enemies closer."

Jewel tried to tell Reagan over and over again that Diamond was still interested in him, but she just charged it to his ego. They had spent almost every day of the past year together, and through all of the drama, Reagan believed that they had found peace and wanted nothing more than to hold onto it.

Jewel got up to lock the door needing a moment to himself. Nothing made him happier than picturing Reagan as his wife, but with everything going on around him, it was hard to remain focused. He grabbed a small glass that sat on the table next to him and filled it half way with the 18-year old scotch his father had given him as a pre-wedding present. He looked around the room saddened that so many people weren't alive to see the day. Sacario graciously agreed to be his best man, but there wasn't a minute that went by that he didn't see Pop's face. It should have been him, but Jewel just accepted that he would be forever haunted. It was his punishment.

Knock. Knock. Knock. Knock.

I swear if this bitch keeps playing with me. "What, Diamond?" he yelled through the thick, wooden door.

"Diamond?" Reagan asked with an attitude.

"Baby, what are you doing here?" he asked pressing his cheek against the door. He wanted nothing more than to fall into the arms of his solitude, but she deserved perfection.

"Open the door," she said jiggling the handle.

"You know I can't do that," he laughed, "Traditions, baby."

"But I want to see you," she whined, "I'm nervous. I need a hug."

"Shit, me too, but I want you walking down the aisle to be the first time I see you. I can't afford for anything to go wrong."

"What could go wrong?"

"Anything, Rea."

"Well, if you feel like that then maybe we should postpone this."

"You sound crazy. $50,000 later, you have no choice but to marry my black ass," he said pausing, "It's not us or you. I can't wait for you to be my wife. I just feel guilty that Pop's not here, you know? Here I am going on with my life while he's lying in a box somewhere."

"Pop would be so proud of you. Not a lot of people get a second chance, Jewel. Remember that."

"You're right, baby," he said hoping her words could soothe him.

"Babe, I hear the music playing, so I guess I should go find your dad. Last chance to back out."

"Not even if you paid me. You're stuck with me, kid. I love you," he said placing his hand on the door.

"I love you too. See you in a minute."

Jewel finished the scotch that was still in his glass before taking one last look in the mirror. It was show time. Preparing himself to marry the love of his life, he grabbed his mango-colored boutonniere and headed for the door. When he opened it, he ran into the last woman he ever expected to see again.

"Mom?" He almost choked on the word as it flew out of his mouth.

"Hi, baby," she said opening her arms wide.

"What are you doing here?"

"Did you think that I would miss the chance to see my only son get married? I wouldn't have missed this for the world," she said walking towards him as she softly grabbed his face, "Aren't you happy to see me?" The coolness of her solid gold rings sent chills through Jewel, but still he said nothing.

"Boy, I know you hear that music," he heard Joe say as he walked back down the hallway, "What's taking so…"

"Hello, Joseph," Laura said with a smirk on her face as he stopped right in his tracks.

"What is she doing here?" he asked turning to Jewel.

"The same reason you are," she said answering for him, "Did you think that I would miss my own son's wedding day?"

"To be honest, yes. I mean you've missed everything else."

"I guess we're in the same damn boat then, huh?"

"Can you guys stop?" Jewel asked putting his head down. Their voices alongside each other reminded him of a time when the arguments were endless, but he refused to be put in the middle again. "First off, Mom, I don't know why you're even here. I haven't seen or talked to you in over ten years. How did you even know that I was here?"

"I have my ways, Jewel. Now can I get a hug, a kiss, something?"

"Ay, Pop's, I'm ready," he said taking a deep breath and smoothing out his jacket, "Mom, I really don't know what your reasons are for being here. I guess I appreciate the effort, but I don't know what you want me to do."

"Baby, we need to talk."

"You can stay if you want," he said ignoring her request, "but I really don't have time for this right now. I'm about to get married."

Jewel walked out of the room leaving the two people responsible for his existence behind. "Why me? I'm a good person," he said staring up at the ceiling as he walked into the sanctuary. When he opened the church doors, the room was packed. He scanned the crowd and saw people he hadn't seen in years. His world had been covered in darkness, so he appreciated the love. As he continued down the aisle, he noticed Golden's family, Isabella, Gabrielle, and Paula sitting right up front.

"You ready?' Sacario asked embracing him as he crept towards the altar. All Jewel could do was shake his head yes.

He was so caught up with Laura being there that he didn't know what to expect. His eyes darted from each entrance and exit searching for her face, but as usual, she was nowhere to be found. Suddenly, the angelic sound of harps being played filled the room. He had waited a long time for this day, and he refused to let it be anything other than perfect. As the music continued to play, the church doors swung open, and everyone turned their heads giving all of their attention to Jailen who carefully walked Chase down the aisle as he held a small white pillow in his hand making sure to complete his task as ring bearer. Chase, oblivious to the formality of the event, giggled his way toward Jewel showing all four of his teeth. Jewel couldn't help but to smile looking at his boys. At that moment, he remembered who it was all for.

"How'd I do, Dad?" Jailen asked standing beside Sacario.

"Perfect," he said kissing him on top of his head.

K-2 and Diamond came walking down the aisle next. Because Gabrielle was pregnant, she didn't mind her taking her place. As Diamond inched closer, she couldn't take her eyes off Jewel. He appeared so king-like standing there awaiting his bride. She just wished that it was her that he was waiting for. Jewel did his best to ignore her lustful stares and put their kiss behind him. All he could think about was Reagan. His palms started to sweat once "Here Comes the Bride" echoed throughout the room and Joe got in position. Reagan was never close with her father, so when Joe graciously offered to walk her down the aisle, how could she say no? With a flowy lace veil covering her face, she took his arm. Jewel couldn't see her staring at him from across the room, but still, she took his breath away. This was their moment. Diamond watched his reaction as she walked down the rose petal-covered aisle. She gripped her bouquet tighter and tighter hating how he couldn't keep his eyes off her. When the music stopped, tears fell down Reagan's cheek as she stood side-by-side with Jewel. He softly grabbed her hand giving it a small squeeze, and at that moment, she had no other choice but to let all of her anxieties and reservations go. He was the one. He always had been.

"Everyone, please be seated," the pastor began, "We are all here today to celebrate the relationship of Reagan Taylor and Jewel Sanchez and the commitment they share together. The bride and groom would like to thank you all for being here and recognize those who couldn't make it here today as they are certainly missed but not forgotten on this day of celebration."

Jewel looked down at the ground. Reagan squeezed his hand back hoping to be the one to calm his nerves this time.

"Marriage gives permanence and structure to a couple's love. It's a way to tell one another that no matter what, 'we're in this together.' A good marriage must be built on a foundation of commitment. The little things are the big things. It's never being too old to hold hands. It's remembering to say, 'I love you' at least once a day. It's never going to sleep angry. It's standing together and facing the world. It's having the capacity to forgive and forget. It's giving each other an atmosphere in which each can grow. It's a common search for the good and the beautiful..."

As the words left the pastor's mouth, Jewel couldn't help but to look over at Reagan and admire her beauty. The formfitting, ivory mermaid gown gripped her hips as it led down to a sea of organza blossoms. She worked hard over the past year to get her body back to where it used to be, and she scrapped her dark locs for her natural honey brown hair. She looked like the girl Jewel had met three years ago in the middle of the darkness in Rain, but she had been his light ever since.

"It's not only about marrying the right partner but also being the right partner," the pastor continued, "The road that has brought Reagan and Jewel here today hasn't been an easy one. It's been filled with challenges that neither were necessarily prepared for, but together, they've taken each one of those experiences and used them to strengthen their love. In 1 Corinthians, Chapter 13, verses 4-8 tells us, 'Love is patient. Love is Kind. It doesn't envy. It does not boast. It is not proud. It is not rude. It's not self-seeking. It is not easily angered. It keeps no record of wrongs. Love does not delight in evil but rejoices in the truth. It always protects, always trusts, always hopes, always perseveres. Love never fails.'"

Reagan and Jewel had definitely been to the bottom. There was so much between them that separated them, but somehow they continued to find their way home. She didn't see what he saw in her until she saw it for herself. He didn't hold her to her past mistakes, so there was no reason why she was stuck on punishing herself. Through all of the fire and chaos with Brandon came a beautiful baby boy, and now, their family was complete. Reagan was thankful.

"Jewel and Reagan will now exchange rings to symbolize their commitment." Jailen stepped forward allowing them to each take the other's ring. "The wearing of these rings is a visible, outward sign that they have committed themselves to one another. Jewel, please take Reagan's hand and repeat these words."

He slowly turned to face her with nothing but a Kool-Aid smile on his face. From the moment he met her, he knew that he wanted to spend the rest of his life with her. He couldn't excuse the pain she put him through, or the pain he put her through, but all he knew was it hurt more to not have her there at all.

"I give you this ring as a symbol of our love."
"I give you this ring as a symbol of our love."
"For today and tomorrow, and for all the days to come."
"For today and tomorrow, and for all the days to come."
"Wear it as a sign of what we promised on this day."
"Wear it as a sign of what we promised on this day."
"And know that my love is present."
"And know that my love is present."
"Even when I'm not."
"Even when I'm not."

"Jewel, you may now place the ring on Reagan's finger." He slid a diamond encrusted band onto her hand matching the rock that was already there.

"Reagan, please take Jewel's hand and repeat these words. I give you this ring as a symbol of our love."

"I give you this ring as a symbol of our love," she said as her voice shook a little.

"For today and tomorrow, and for all the days to come."
"For today and tomorrow, and for all the days to come."
"Wear it as a sign of what we promised on this day."
"Wear it as a sign of what we promised on this day."

"And know that my love is present."

"And know that my love is present."

"Even when I am not."

"Even when I am not." As soon as the last word left her lips, Reagan slipped Jewel's solid white gold band on his finger officially making him hers for life.

"By sharing your vows and exchanging rings here today, you both have decided, under the one true God, to share the rest of your lives together. You are no longer two separate people but now one couple together. Reagan, do you take Jewel to be your husband, to live together in the sanctity of marriage? Do you promise to love him, comfort him, honor and keep him in sickness and in health, and forsaking all others for as long as you both shall live?"

"I do," she said without question.

"Jewel, do you take Reagan to be your wife, to live together in the sanctity of marriage? Do you promise to love her, comfort her, honor and keep her in sickness and in health, and forsaking all others for as long as you both shall live?"

"I do," he said ignoring Diamond's resentful glances.

"If anyone objects to this marriage, please speak now or forever hold your peace," the pastor said scanning the room. Jewel's eyes immediately shot over to her. If she ruined this day for him, he didn't know what he'd do. "By the power vested in me, I now pronounce you husband and wife. Jewel, you may now kiss your bride."

Forgetting that the world even existed, he grabbed Reagan in his arms as she melted into his embrace. He lifted her veil already knowing the gift that awaited him underneath, but still her beauty blew him away.

"I love you," he said lightly kissing her on the lips.

"I love you too," she said wiping the tears from her eyes. She felt fireworks once their lips touched.

"It's my great honor and privilege to be the first to present to you Mr. and Mrs. Jewel Noah Sanchez."

Hand-in-hand, they walked down the aisle receiving all of the love from their family and friends. They finally did it.

After they got to the back of the church, Joe rushed to meet them.

"Is my mom still here?" Jewel hurried to ask.

"Mom?" Reagan looked up at him in confusion.

"No, thank God, but she told me to give you this," Joe said handing him a business card. In black ink that bled across the white card stock was an unfamiliar phone number, but Jewel recognized the New York area code all too well.

"J, please tell me what's going on."

"My mom showed up just before the ceremony started," he said playing with the card with his thumb.

"What she say?"

"That we needed to talk."

"Are you gonna call her?"

"I don't know yet. I mean what could she possibly have to say now?"

Chapter 2

The next day, K-2 found himself back at home in bed with Gabrielle tucked in his arms. She was eight-months pregnant, and he was loving every minute of it. While she was dealing with all of the aches and pains, he was picking out baby names, buying clothes and furniture for the nursery, signing them up for prenatal classes. He was ready to go all out. This was his first child, and the fact that he was actually in love with Gabrielle meant a lot to him. He felt like he was finally doing something right for a change. Because of her energy level, she was taking a few online classes to stay busy. She learned a lot of game from her dad, but with a business degree behind her, she knew she could take Rich City Cutz to the next level whether K-2 wanted her to or not.

"You going to the shop today?" she asked rolling over and placing a small kiss on his lips.

"Yeah, I'm bout to get up now," he said bending over the bed to check his phone that sat on the floor, "Ay, you need to sit at the desk or something." The bed was covered with scattered notebooks, pens, pencils, and different colored highlighters as she sat with her laptop right next to her.

"For what?" she asked still glued to the screen.

"All that radiation ain't good for my lil mama, man."

"Here you go."

"Yeah, here I go," K-2 mocked, "I was reading this book..."

"I wish you would read a book about how to get some business cause I got this."

"You and that baby are my business."

"I swear you gon' worry yourself to death."

"If something happens to my baby, Gabrielle, I'ma kick your ass."

"If this baby comes out looking like an octopus, you better still love it," she laughed.

"Shhiiittttt," he said jumping out of the bed, "Maury gon' be like, 'You are not the father.'"

"Forreal, what you bout to do today?"

"What I do every day. GTM. Get this money."

"Well, you have three interviews this afternoon. One for a new female stylist. I've seen her work. She's dope, and two new barbers. I already emailed you their resumes, so please try and skim through them when you get to the shop. I'm not tryna hear your mouth about how you don't like these mothafuckas too."

"I will. I promise," K-2 said finally walking into the bathroom.

$$$$$

After showering, shaving, and grabbing a quick bite to eat, he made his way down to the shop. He felt on top of the world. His girl and home were provided for, and he had his own. Some days he missed being on the block with his boys, but he already knew where that future would lead him. As he pulled into the parking lot, he saw a swarm of black and white police cars surrounding his shop. The sea of red and blue lights reflected off of the glass illuminating the yellow police tape covering the building.

"Yo, what the fuck is this?" he asked jumping out of his truck.

"Sir, please step back," an officer said blocking him from his path.

"Man, fuck all that. This is my shop, man. What happened?"

"Sir, please follow me," he said leading him away from the crime scene, but K-2 couldn't keep his eyes off the shattered glass that covered the concrete.

"Are you Keith Tu, sir?" a detective in a brown coat asked.

"Yeah."

"Well, it looks like your store front was shot up earlier this morning."

"I can see that," he said noticing several bullet holes in the wall. As much as he hated the police, he had to find out what happened.

"We've spoken to a few witnesses around the neighborhood who believe this to be gang related."

"Gang related?" he asked more to himself. He had been done with the M.A.C. Boys for a while now, so he couldn't think of who was sending warning shots.

"Do you have any idea who could have done this?"

"Do I look like I do? Don't assume that just because you see a young black male out here shining that he's banging."

"I never said that, sir. I just..."

"Listen, I have insurance, so no further investigation is needed on my part. I mean it's Richmond. Shit happens," K-2 said turning to walk away.

"But sir, this is why this sort of thing continues to happen. We need the support of the community. It has to be a team effort."

"I appreciate your concern, officer, but your help is not needed," he said again before disappearing into the shop.

Despite the police still scurrying around outside, K-2 went to the back to his office. Nothing was stolen or broken. Only the front window was shot out. He had to figure out his next steps, and the only person he could think to call was Sacario.

"Hello?"

"Ay, where you at?"

"At the house bout to go meet up with Hassan. What's up?"

"So I had a couple interviews scheduled for today, which I now have to cancel," he said reminding himself, "I call myself going down to the shop early to look over some resumes cause Gabrielle has been on my ass, whatever, whatever. Blood, tell me why when I got down here, the whole store front was shot the fuck out?"

"What?"

"Glass and police were everywhere. Nothing else is fucked up except a couple bullet holes in the wall outside."

"So what's next?"

"Bruh, you tell me."

"Kiko's here. I'ma call you in a minute. I don't need her tryna wrap herself in this shit too."

"I got you," K-2 said hanging up.

"Who was that?" she asked walking into the kitchen.

"Your crazy-ass brother."

"I feel like I haven't seen him in forever. What was he talking about?"

"Shit, work. You know how he is now."

"I never thought that I would see the day when he would got his shit together, you know? Especially not running around with your ass, but I'm really proud of him. Our whole family is."

"Yeah, me too," Sacario said looking down at the ground.

"What's the look for?"

"What look?"

"Sacario, I know that look. What's really going on?"

"Nothing," he said grabbing the bottom of her face placing a kiss on her lips, "Can it just be nothing?"

"Yeah, just not with you," she said giving him the side eye.

After he was arrested, Kiko attached herself to him even more. She wanted to be involved in the M.A.C. Boys, but Sacario refused. To him, her first and only responsibility was to be a mom to their 4-year old daughter Arianna, but she was bored being a housewife. She needed some excitement in her life.

"Listen, you need to get a hobby or something. I know that you worry, but this time isn't like last time, okay? I will never put you or Ari in that position ever again. I just need you to trust me."

"Okay," she said relaxing a little.

"You tryna go to Sac this weekend?"

"For what?"

"Well, I felt bad that Jewel didn't let me throw him a bachelor party, so I'ma do it up one time for my bruh."

"I think I'll pass."

"Why are you so anti-social?"

"I'm not anti-social. I just don't know them like that."

"Now's your chance. Jewel's girl has a 1-year old, and you know Ari already thinks she's somebody's mama. It's gon' be cool. A little family day."

"I don't know, Sacario."

"Kiko, how much am I around your family and your friends? I'm just asking for one day."

"Okay," she said not wanting to fight. She was very protective, and she didn't like adding new people to her circle, but she knew how much of an impact the M.A.C. Boys had on Sacario's life, so she decided to go with the flow. "What day?"

"Saturday, so clear your schedule."

"Where are we going?"

"Nope, no more questions. I just need you to show up."

"You know I don't like surprises."

"Well, good thing this shit ain't for you then, huh?" he said kissing her on the cheek, "I'm bout to go link up with Hassan. I'll be back later, okay?"

"Yeah," Kiko said following him to the door. No matter where he went, she hated feeling like there was a chance that he wouldn't make it home again. She didn't think she'd ever get used to it.

"I'm still picking up Arianna from daycare, right?"

"Yeah, I have my workout class later."

"Alright, you know Jewel's wife owns her own gym, right? See ya'll have something in common already."

"Stop it."

"Love you."

"Love you too," she said watching him walk to his car. He hurried hoping not to draw any more attention to himself.

When he got the call from K-2, he already knew who was behind the shooting. The M.A.C. Boys was getting bigger in the Bay, and a lot of people didn't like that, but since K-2 was out of the game, Sacario knew they would be gunning for him first.

"Where you at, bruh?" he asked pulling out of the driveway.

"The house. Why, what's up?"

"I'm on my way right now."

"Yep," Hassan said hanging up the phone.

Sacario and Hassan had been friends ever since middle school. Hassan was always on the straight and narrow path, but he never lost sight of where he came from. After graduating from Howard University a few years back, he moved back to the Bay, and they became attached at the hip again. When Jewel announced that he was leaving the M.A.C. Boys for good, and then K-2, Sacario couldn't think of a better person to have by his side. Hassan was finding work harder and harder to come by even with his Bachelor's Degree in Film Studies, so soon, getting money with his brother didn't seem that bad.

Twenty minutes later, he pulled up to an all-white townhouse in Hilltop. A box Chev, a Lexus, and a Navigator were all parked out in front. Sacario ran up the long flight of stairs that led to the front door, but before he could knock, Hassan opened it.

"What do I owe this early morning visit?" he smiled.

"K's shop got hit."

"I heard," Hassan admitted. Word around town traveled fast. "Where's he at?"

"At the shop still I think."

"You know who did it, right?"

"I wanna say them niggas off 23rd Street."

"Yep, they disrespectful with it too, bruh. That M.A.C. shit don't sit too well out here, but all you gotta do is give me the word, and it's handled."

"You know what to do," Sacario said sitting down as he eased a blunt from behind his ear.

Hassan walked to the back room giving his orders as second-in-command. Sacario wasn't above clapping back, but for the sake of his family, he tried not to get his hands dirty anymore. He could overhear Hassan barking orders into the phone like a general to their young hitters. He knew that there would be some resistance with the M.A.C. Boys making their presence known more and more in the Bay, but he was ready. He didn't care what Jewel and K-2 had decided to do; he would let the game decide when it was done with him.

"Problem solved," Hassan said walking back into the living room, "You sure you don't wanna go down there yourself?"

"What, you don't trust Armani and PJ?"

"Naw, don't get me wrong, it's not that. I would just prefer to know that this shit gets handled. We can't afford to get caught slipping."

"I feel you, Sani, I do, but I gotta let these little niggas do their job. That's what I pay them for. If we need to step in, we will, but I have faith in my team."

"Well, that frees up my day a little then. What you tryna do?"

"I need to link up with K to make sure he's straight. You tryna ride?"

"Yeah, let me grab my hat," Hassan said walking into his bedroom. "Where Chyna at?"

"Who?" he yelled.

"Blood, don't act like that," Sacario said laughing.

"Man, I had to give that bitch them walking papers. She was a headache."

"What happened?" he asked getting up.

"Shit was cool, but then she got a little bit too comfortable. We weren't even together for three months, and she was already asking me to pay her rent, her car note, her cell phone bill. The money was never an issue, so I helped her out a few times with shit here and there, but then it got to a point where I was like, 'Hold on, lil baby, I ain't your nigga.'"

"She was tryna get wifed up one time," Sacario said laughing again.

"Yep, but by the wrong one," Hassan said locking the front door, "I'm cool on these basic-ass females. I don't need a bitch to take care of me, but it would be nice if one came to the table with at least a plate."

"Let me hook you up with one of Kiko's potnahs."

"It's good, bruh. This ain't the *Love Connection*," he said walking down the stairs towards Sacario's car. K-2's shop was only around the corner, so within a few minutes, they were there.

When they pulled up, men in black jumpsuits circled around the front of the shop with *Wilkins' Glass Repair* etched across their backs. Sacario spotted K-2 from the corner of his eye as he walked around the parking lot with the sun shining down on his face.

"Damn, that was fast, nigga," Hassan said motioning toward the new, spotless glass window.

"I don't have time to wait. What I look like having my front window shot out? That's bad for business."

"Don't you have insurance?"

"Yeah, I'll just submit all my receipts later, but what's up? You got some news for me?"

"Let's go inside," Sacario said nodding his head towards the repairmen who whirled around the parking lot.

"Ay, if ya'll need me, I'll be in the back," K-2 yelled over his shoulder.

"Sure thing."

"So what's up, man? You making me nervous," he said walking inside.

"It was them niggas off 23rd. I told you how Jay got into it with them last week, right?"

"Yeah," K-2 said wanting Sacario to get to the point.

"Jay was with his girl, and that one nigga Freddy from 2-3 got at her hella disrespectful. Jay was ready to put a hot one in him, but he was tryna be cool for his girl's sake, you know?"

"So you telling me I'm still pulling glass out of my ass for a stunt?"

"Naw, man," Hassan chimed in, "After a few words were exchanged, the dudes realized that Jay was with M.A.C. I told Sacario that people ain't liking that too much. They tried Jay with that fake shit, and of course he beat they ass, so I'm thinking this shit here was retaliation."

"So what now? What's the plan of action?"

"I sent the goonies out that way earlier," Hassan said wanting to reassure him.

"That's it?"

"What you mean that's it?" Sacario asked, "What you want me to do? Blow they house up or something?"

"Yeah, or something, nigga. I got my family to think about."

"K, I got this. They obviously ain't about that life or they would have hit more than some glass. Armani and PJ are handling the shit as we speak."

"Man, I don't know," he said putting his head in his hands.

"Have I ever let you down?" Sacario asked in all seriousness.

"Naw, never," K-2 admitted.

"And I don't plan on it now, bruh. Just trust me, okay?"

"Alright, blood."

"Plus, I got something that will take your mind off of all this bullshit."

"What?"

"Being that Jewel has been on his square shit lately, this weekend, I'ma surprise him with the bachelor party he should've had."

"Don't you think it's a little too late for that, Cari, blood?"

"He doesn't really have a choice at this point. I was his best man, and he didn't allow me to do my best man shit. I'm owed this."

"How you sound?" K-2 laughed, "And you know he ain't gon' go nowhere without Reagan."

"I already got that covered. Kiko and Ari are coming down too. You can bring Gabby if you want."

"I don't know, man. She ain't gon' be trying to go to the club or no shit."

"Well, she can go to her parents' house if she wants to. I don't really give a fuck, but you better be there."

"Who you bringing, Sani?"

"Myself."

"What happened to Chyna, blood?"

"Long story."

"Fuck it then. After I get this shit squared away, I'm fa sho gon' be free."

"It's set then. This weekend, we blasting out to Sac."

Chapter 3

"Jewel, did I leave Chase's diaper bag down there?" Reagan yelled from the top of the stairs.

"Yeah, I think I saw it in the kitchen," he said before continuing with his conversation with Joe, "Sorry, that was Reagan."

"How she doing?"

"Good, she's about to go to work."

"Already?"

"Yep."

After getting pregnant with Chase, Reagan gained over fifty pounds. She hated how the birth of her son completely changed her body, but with that frustration, she became motivated to lose the weight. She loved being a mother and spending time with her son meant the world to her, but she wasn't willing to forget about herself in the process, so she found ways to workout with him. Soon, she fell in love with being healthy and fit, and it became second nature. Within six months, Reagan was in the best shape of her life, and other new mothers around the neighborhood began to take notice. They all wanted to know her secret. Reagan was flattered, but she just saw it as another way of spending time with her baby. The weight loss benefits were just extra, but Jewel saw it as a business opportunity. As long as he had known her, she never had her own. Whether it was Styles and then later him, she always had someone to take care of her financially. Jewel didn't mind providing for his family, but he thought that it was time for her to finally grow up, so he bought her a small gym facility and helped turn into *Baby 'n Me Fitness*. Reagan was able to take her and Chase's routine and sell it to women all across the city. At first it took her some getting used to because she never had to work a day in her life, but she fell in love with her independence. She never knew what her passions were while being with Styles, but for Jewel, it was important for her to find out.

"What about the honeymoon?"

"I mean we're still gonna go I guess. I stupidly bought us tickets to Bora Bora only to have her tell me that she's too busy this month," Jewel sighed.

"She's spoiled, son," Joe said laughing.

"Who you telling? But I can't lie, her little business has been doing really good. Her classes are constantly full, so she hired a few more instructors."

"And the babies are in the actual classes?"

"Yeah, the whole idea behind it was that a lot of new moms feel like they don't have time to work out because taking care of a newborn is hella time consuming, so she has these workouts that are like a little over thirty minutes or something like that for different age groups. I guess they like that they don't have to stick the kids in like a daycare situation while they're there. She's thinking about adding a juice bar next."

"Gabby probably would like something like that once she has Navaeh," Joe said thinking out loud, "You know I'm really proud of Reagan."

"Yeah, she's been doing her thing. It's different, but it's definitely something positive in her life. Jailen even goes up there with her and Chase sometimes to help out too."

"Speaking of Jailen, how are things going with you and Diamond?"

"The same. I mean it's frustrating because that's the mother of my son, and I love her, don't get me wrong. I care about her health, her wellbeing, all of that shit, but she refuses to acknowledge that I'm not in love with her. I have no romantic feelings towards her whatsoever, but she wants me to. A while ago, I told her that I would help her with a down payment on a house since she has joint custody of J now. We're supposed to be going to look at a few places today. He deserves his own space while he's with Diamond, and that small-ass apartment ain't gon' cut it. With her working again, I know that she's more stable at this point."

"So what's the problem?"

"Her and this Reagan bullshit. She acts like they're really best friends or something, but it's only another opportunity for her to be in my face."

"Have a little faith, Jewel."

"I think my faith is dead."

"Everything done in the dark will always come to the light, remember that. I love Reagan. You know I do, but she's very naïve. A very sweet girl but naïve. It's only going to cause tension between you two if you keep trying to expose Diamond. Her true intentions will become clear with time, and Reagan will be able to make her decision about her for herself. Don't drive yourself crazy, son." Jewel took a deep breath and sighed heavily into the phone. "I know that things have been rough lately with your new transition and all, but I want you to know that I'm very proud of you."

"Thanks, Pop," Jewel said sitting back against the couch. He put so much pressure on himself that it was nice when someone else recognized his sacrifices sometimes.

"So have you talked to your mom yet?"

"Nope."

"Do you plan on talking to your mom?"

"I don't know," he admitted, "I mean what she could possibly have to say?"

"Well, Jewel, you won't know until you find out. I can only speak from my own experience, but I didn't know if I would ever see you again to be honest, but the night I ran into you, I knew that it was more than just a coincidence. God was finally giving me the chance to make things right again, but if it wasn't for your forgiveness, I wouldn't be sitting here on the phone with you talking about your day."

"I know what you're saying," he said putting his head down, "It wasn't easy to forgive you, believe me, and I don't anticipate this being easy either. For over ten years, I hated you two. I didn't understand how it got to the point where I didn't talk to you guys anymore. You didn't know where I was, and I didn't know where ya'll were. It was like you just disappeared."

"That's exactly how it felt too. You know I'm not a fan of your mother, but all I can say is maybe it won't hurt to hear her out. She tracked you down for a reason."

"I'm glad you said that."

"What?"

"I want you to be there with me when I talk to her."

"Me?"

"Not just you but Isabella and Gabrielle too. If I have to come to terms with this lady then I think it's only fair that you do too. Let's just put everything out on the table once and for all."

"If me being there will help you finally heal, son, then I'm there. It's not gonna be easy, but I'm ready to atone for my past."

"Thanks, Pops, this really means a lot to me."

"Anything for you, son. Call me later with the details."

"I will."

"Love you, man."

"Love you too," Jewel said before hanging up.

"Alright, let me get out of here," Reagan said walking into the room. The bright turquoise sports bra and black tights she wore hugged her in all the right places.

"Can I get a kiss before you skip your ass out of here?" he asked feeling neglected.

"I'm sorry, baby," she said slowing down a bit. Being a new business owner was exciting, but she didn't want to jeopardize her marriage in the process. She set Chase down letting him run around for a while as she sat down next to Jewel.

"Any word on the trip yet?"

"Two weeks," she said kissing him on the lips.

"Two weeks is all you need?"

"Yep."

"In fourteen days, you'll be ready for a few weeks with no kids, no gym, and especially no Diamond?"

"Stop it," Reagan said punching him in the arm, "In two weeks, I will be all yours. I'm sorry that I haven't been around these past few months. I mean we just got married two days ago, and already, we're back to our everyday lives, but I've never found something that I liked and I was good at before. At first, after I had Chase, I just wanted to lose weight for superficial reasons of course, but after he was old enough and I could take him with me when I worked out, it became about our time together. Through my own journey with my baby, I'm able to help other women see that strong, vibrant, resilient woman that is still within them. It took me a long time to find her myself, and now that I have, I'm never letting go."

"I just miss you. That's all. Don't ever think that I'm not proud of you because I am. I guess I just need to find my own thing again, you know?"

"And you will, Jewel. You're not even thirty yet…"

"Shit, damn near."

"Stop pressuring yourself. You still have time to go back to the drawing board. It's never too late."

"Yeah, I guess."

"Anyway, enough about all that. What you got planned for today?" Reagan asked wanting to change the subject. Ever since Pop's death and Jewel's departure from the M.A.C. Boys, he hadn't been the same.

"I'm bout to go look at a few places with Diamond."

"Yeah, she told me she found some close by."

"And that doesn't bother you?"

"No, not really. It would make the kids going back and forth easier. I know that you two have your issues, but we're in a good place, okay? And I want to keep it like that."

Jewel refused to say anything else on the matter. If Reagan needed to touch the fire to see that it really was hot then he was prepared for her to get burned.

"You're right, baby," he said getting up and kissing her on her forehead, "Let me grab Chase's bag, so you can get out of here."

"So what was Joe talking about?" she asked following behind him.

"Me, you, my mom," he said nonchalantly.

"Have you talked to her yet?" she asked not wanting to push Jewel. She knew how sensitive he was when it came to Laura.

"Nope," he repeated.

"Do you plan to?"

"You sound just like Joe."

"Jewel, I know that seeing your mom after all that time was probably crazy, but maybe actually talking to her will give you some sort of clarity." He was losing his mind being away from the life he had surrounded himself with for so many years. Although she knew it was for the better, she couldn't help but notice how lost he really was.

"You're right again, Rea. That's the reason why I needed to talk to my pops. I do want to see what my mom has to say, but it's been so long since I've even seen her. I just don't want to get cornered like I did with Joe, you know? It was a lot to take in all at once. This time, I want things to be on my terms."

"So what's the solution then?"

"Joe, Isabella, and Gabrielle are all gonna be there whenever we meet."

"Don't you think that will make the situation even tenser?" Reagan asked shaking her head at the messiness.

"Oh, well, these mothafuckas put me through hell, so now it's time for them to come face-to-face with that, and plus, if my mom is on that weird shit, I'll have a scapegoat fa sho."

"Jewel, you know you wrong," she said laughing as she finally grabbed Chase's diaper bag before placing him back on her hip.

Ding. Dong. Ding. Dong. Ding. Dong.

"That's probably Diamond," Jewel said rolling his eyes.

"I'll get it." Reagan walked towards the door, and when she opened it, Jailen flew inside.

"I thought…you left me," he said almost out of breath.

"You know I couldn't leave my number one employee. You ready?"

"Yep."

"Where's your bag?"

"In the car. I'll be right back. Don't leave," he said running out of the house again.

"Hey, girl," Diamond said kissing Reagan on the cheek, "You look cute today."

"Well, since it's almost summer and all, I thought that I would brighten things up a little," she said spinning around.

"Go head, hot mama."

"Anyway, let me get them out of here. Ya'll enjoy your day, and I'll see you later," Reagan said kissing Jewel on the lips before walking outside to meet Jailen.

"You ready or what?" Diamond asked catching an attitude.

"Don't start," he said walking into the kitchen to grab his keys, "I'm tryna have a cool day, so let's just get this over with."

"Don't say it like that. You acting like you don't wanna even come." She couldn't help but roll her eyes.

"Acting? I'm not acting. Diamond, we don't need to be all up under each other twenty-four seven. I'm not your nigga, but I'm really starting to realize that you don't understand that."

"Jewel, how could I not? I just watched you get married to that bitch. How do you think I feel?"

"So why are you here?" he asked turning to face her, "If I was you, I wouldn't put myself through no shit like that."

"I stupidly thought that we could be around each other for more than five seconds without you hating me."

"You know what? I do hate you," Jewel snapped.

"Listen, I know last year was rough, but…"

"Rough? How do I think our son felt not having you here for weeks on end because you were out taking lines off that white boy's dick? Or how do you think I felt having six months of my life snatched away from me just to have you go back to that nigga?"

"Jewel, I…"

"I don't care anymore. You are no longer my problem, Diamond. I'm obligated to take care of my son, and that's it. Yes, my life was messy, and unfortunately, you and Jailen were casualties in it, but I never meant for that to happen. It just did. I wanted to work on keeping our family together, but that wasn't important to you. You let us go without even thinking twice."

"Don't say that," Diamond said with tears slowly streaming down her cheeks, "I never wanted to let you go. I love you. I want to be with you."

"If you did then you would've stayed."

"That's not fair," she yelled, "Can you really say that if I would've stayed, we would be together right now?"

"Yes."

"What about Reagan?"

"What about Reagan?"

"If we would have stayed together, you still would've ran into her, and your feelings for her would've still been the same. Can you honestly look me in the eye and say that you wouldn't have gone back to her?"

"I don't know," Jewel said wanting to spare her feelings. His heart always belonged to Reagan even when he was with Diamond, but she knew that.

"You're a fucking lair," she said wiping her eyes, "You never loved me like you loved her, but I still don't get it though."

"Get what?"

"What you actually see in her. What type of nigga wants to shack up with a bitch after only seeing her a couple of times? You plotted on her, and she cheated on her nigga to be with you. What type of bitch is that?"

"You don't know what you're talking about. She never cheated."

"That time, right? My bad, but then she goes and not only leaves you to fuck on your best friend, but then she gets pregnant by the nigga too. She's hella trifling, but you wifed that," she said looking at him with disgust, "How does it feel to have another man's baby calling you daddy?"

She was hurt. Over the past year, she was able to clean herself up and place her focus back on their son. She would be lying if she said she didn't regret ending it with Jewel and losing their family, but deep down, she knew it was inevitable. She loved him, but he could never love her the way he loved Reagan, and she hated him for that.

"You know what? Get out. You're not my bitch, so who I deal with is who I deal with. I don't owe you no mothafucking explanation," Jewel said opening the front door.

"Are you serious? What about the house?"

"Hold on," he said digging in his pocket and pulling out his wallet, "As long as I don't have to fucking talk to you anymore, we're all good. I'll call Paula when I pick up or drop off Jailen from now on. This back and forth bullshit is for the birds." He ripped a blank check from his check book, and after signing the bottom line, he flicked it outside the door.

"I really don't care what the place costs, just leave me the fuck alone," he spat as he closed the door behind him.

"Fuck you, nigga," Diamond said reluctantly picking up the small piece of paper from the warm concrete, "You always think you can just throw money at your problems. You're really no different from Marcus..."

"Like I said before, you are not my problem anymore," he said opening up the door again, "That's for my son. I wanted us to be cool, co-parent, and all the shit, but at the same time, I'm not tryna give you false hope. I don't want you around me or my wife. Stay away from her, Diamond. I'm serious."

"Tell that bitch to stay away from me," she said walking back to her car.

Ring. Ring. Ring. Ring. Ring. Ring. Ring. Ring.

Jewel placed his hands on top of his head and took a deep breath. He felt the muscles in his neck and shoulders tense up as he tried to remain calm. Diamond used to be his peace, but now she was just his headache.

Ring. Ring. Ring. Ring. Ring. Ring. Ring. Ring.

His cellphone continued to ring in his pocket. The muffled sound echoed throughout the house as he walked upstairs to his room.

"Hello," he said before reaching the top of the stairs.

"Nigga, I've been calling you all morning," Sacario said.

"My bad, blood, I've been dealing with some bullshit today."

"Diamond?"

"Bruh, who else?"

"When you and Reagan going on your honeymoon?"

"In like two weeks."

"That's perfect."

"Why, what's up?"

"Me and K-2 were tryna slide out there this weekend. I thought we would bring the fam."

"That's what's up." It had been a while since he had been around his potnahs, so the break was much needed.

"I was planning to shoot out there like Saturday morning and then leave Sunday night. I guess Gabrielle's mom is throwing her a surprise baby shower Sunday, and K-2 wants Kiko and Arianna to go."

"I didn't even know about it," he said laughing, "Isabella don't be telling my pops shit."

"That's cold."

"He'll end up just telling Gabrielle. It happens every time. She be playing the fuck out of that old-ass nigga," he laughed again, "I'll be here though."

"Alright, bruh, I'll hit you when we're on our way."

"Yep."

"Oh, yeah, I got my boy Hassan coming up too. I need to holla at you about some business."

"It's good."

"Alright."

"One," Jewel said hanging up the phone. After everything that happened, he appreciated that he still had friends in Sacario and K-2. He carried the weight of Golden and Pop's death on his shoulders every day. He had to look into Chase's face only to see Brandon's, and Diamond refused to let him go. Being able to chill with his real family was what he needed to turn his mind off for just a little while.

He laid down on his bed letting the silence soothe him as he played with the white card that sat in his pocket like he did every day since he got it. Curiosity held him prisoner as he tried to imagine what his mother had to say, but fear always got the best of him before he found out. With Joe now on board for their impromptu family reunion, he tried to develop his nerve. He pulled the business card out of his pocket and studied the phone number written on the front. His hand shook as he finally dialed the familiar digits. It was either now or never.

"Laura Smith speaking," she said answering on the first ring. Jewel remained silent as the call filled with dead air. He had so much to say, but he just couldn't get the words out. "Hello?"

"Hey, ummm....this is Jewel."

"Jewel, baby? I'm so glad you called. I know that your wedding day was probably the wrong place to just pop up after all this time, but, son, I really need to talk to you."

"I agree, Mom, it has been a long time, and I think I'm finally ready, but before I commit to anything, I want you to know that I asked Joe to be there too. Putting your relationship aside, I just think that it would benefit everyone if we put everything out on the table."

Laura didn't say anything. To her, Joe was spineless, and she still couldn't stand the sight of him, but at that point, she was willing to do anything to reconnect with her son.

"Okay, if that's what you need, Jewel, then that's fine with me. What day works best for you?"

"How's Friday?"

"That's perfect. I'm back in New York, but I'll be on the first thing out of here Thursday morning. I've really missed you, Jewel."

"It's been a long time," he said not knowing what else to say. As much as he resented his father in the past for not being there, he resented Laura even more. He never understood how a mother could just give up on her child.

"Well, I guess I'll see you Friday."

"See you Friday," he said hanging up and laying back down on the bed. He didn't know if he was really ready for what was about to come next.

$$\$\$\$\$\$$$

Reagan walked into the house with Chase asleep on her shoulder and Jailen by her side. The hours of basketball he insisted on playing with some of the older kids had him dead to the world, and all he could think about was his bed. She followed behind him up the stairs to Chase's room where she put him down for bed. She had their schedule down pat, so she knew they both would be sleep for the rest of the night. After making sure they were all tucked in, she walked into her and Jewel's room, but he was nowhere to be found. She walked downstairs and opened the door that led to their garage. His car was gone.

"They can't still be looking at houses," she said looking up at the clock as she pulled out her cellphone. The bright screen illuminated the kitchen as she dialed Jewel's number, but the phone just rang and rang. Irritated by his lack of communication, she decided to call Diamond.

"Hello?" she said answering on the first ring. She was convinced that Reagan had found out about her fight with Jewel.

"Hey, girl, is Jewel still with you?"

"Jewel?" she asked confused, "The last time I saw that nigga was right before he kicked me out of his house."

"Wait, what?" Reagan asked walking into the living room to sit down.

"He didn't tell you?"

"Me and the kids just got home. I haven't talked to him all day. What happened?"

"After you guys left, he just had this bad-ass attitude from jump. I tried to see what the issue was, and he flashed."

"What was he saying?"

"The usual. He was telling me how much he hates me, and he kept bringing up me and Marcus, and how I'm such a terrible mother."

"I told him to cool it with that shit. I mean this tension between ya'll isn't good for Jailen, you know?"

"Try telling Jewel that. I swear he's set on making me pay for my mistakes, but I mean we were able to get past our bullshit, so I don't know why me and him can't."

"You're Jailen's mother, and that's never gonna change. Jewel is going through a lot with this transition and everything. He's just frustrated."

"Yeah, I guess."

"So what happened with the house then if ya'll never left?"

"He threw a blank check at me and was like he didn't care how much it cost as long as I leave you and him alone, but I don't feel right spending his money like that."

"He is so dramatic," Reagan said rolling her eyes, "I'll fix this."

"I don't think Borgia himself could fix this shit, but call me later."

"I will," she said hanging up the phone. She hated always being in the middle of their drama, but he was her husband, and she considered Diamond a friend. In a perfect world, they would all be able to peacefully co-exist and raise Jailen together, but in their world, nothing was ever perfect.

Sasha Ravae

As Reagan sat deep in her frustrations, the front door swung open and in walked Jewel carrying a few bags in his hand. She walked into the unlit area of the foyer as he closed the door.

"Damn, I was tryna beat ya'll here. I got us some tacos," he said leaning in for a kiss, but Reagan backed away. "Like that?" he asked turning on the lights, "What I do now?"

"Please tell me that you didn't kick Diamond out of our house and throw a check at her," she said folding her arms across her chest.

"Rea, don't start. You don't know Diamond like you think you do," he said walking into the kitchen to put the food down on the counter, "She deserved that shit."

"Why? Jewel, you fail to realize that you're tied to this woman for the rest of your life. Why spend all that time being miserable? I understand that all that shit she did last year affected both you and Jailen, but at what point do you start forgiving her? She's not the same person anymore."

All he could do was laugh. "Are you serious? Please don't tell me that was the sob story she gave you."

"Yeah, she said that after I left, you just started tripping, bringing up her and Marcus..."

"Listen, I'm not over here thinking about Diamond and her past indiscretions. As hard as it may be to believe, I'm tryna move forward with my life, and in my opinion, she doesn't fit into that. When she came over today, she instantly caught an attitude."

"Why though?"

"Because we're married," Jewel yelled.

"When I left, she seemed fine."

"Rea, you can't be that stupid. She wants what you have. I don't see how you can't see that. She's been on some fatal attraction-type shit. After all of her ploys to convince me to leave your big headed-ass alone and go back to her, I lost it, so yes, I did throw a check at her and told her to leave. Then I went to my dad's, and then I went about my night and got some tacos. I'm not thinking about Diamond, Reagan. I just wish you weren't either."

"Jewel, I am a grown-ass woman. I can be around who I want to be around. Yeah, me and Diamond have had our ups and downs, but right now, we're good."

"Reagan, I get that you never really got over losing Robyn the way you did, but believe me, she is no substitution. Diamond is not your friend. If I told her today that I wanted our family to be back together,

32

she wouldn't think twice about you. I told her to stay away from you, and I'm serious."

"You're not gonna tell me who I can be friends with, Jewel."

"You heard what I said," he said before grabbing a few tacos and heading upstairs.

Chapter 4

Four Days Later...

"Why you tryna stay in Sac all weekend if we're just going to this thing with Jewel tonight?" Gabrielle asked getting dressed, "I have homework to do."

"Would you just chill?" K-2 said throwing his dark blue Polo over his head, "Sacario said he's throwing Jewel and Reagan something like a surprise wedding party tomorrow night, so I figured we just stay til Sunday if that's okay with you?"

"I mean I guess it has to be since you make plans without telling me," she said rolling her eyes.

"Here you go."

"So what else haven't you told me, Keith?"

"What?" The question caught him off guard.

"What else haven't you told me? It's not calculus, nigga. You shouldn't have to figure out your answer."

"Man, I don't know what you're talking about," he said spraying *The One* along his ear and neck.

"Oh, ok, well, I talked to Kiko last night."

"Ok, and?"

"And she told me what happened down at the shop."

"Damn, how she find out?"

"Does it matter?" Gabrielle asked becoming angry. She wanted to believe that they were building this fairytale life together, but it was obvious that K-2's past was always lurking somewhere in the shadows. "I thought you were done with all this shit, Keith?"

"I am, but I can't help what these niggas do out of retaliation. I mean just because I got out the game doesn't mean I disappeared."

"I wanna move."

"Gabby, we're not moving. Would you relax please? Do you think that I would put you, my future wife or our unborn daughter in danger like that? The shop getting shot up was just some fluke shit, but it's been handled. I know what I want, and that's our family. I'm not ready to give that up. You believe me?" he asked kissing her belly.

"Yes," she said rubbing the short waves that covered his head. She was in love with him, but there wasn't a day that went by that she didn't think about Pop. She didn't want the same thing happening to K-2.

Counterfeit *Dreams* 4

$$$$$

For the past four days, Reagan walked around the house giving Jewel the silent treatment, and soon he fell into the silence. He knew what Diamond's true motives were, and he just wanted to protect her, but Reagan was stubborn. She was set on making her own mistakes, and as much as he didn't want to, he had to let her.

"I'm sorry," he finally said as he walked into their room. Reagan sat on the bed with her back facing him as she continued to get dressed for work. "I know that you're mad, but I need you to know that I will do whatever I can to protect you, but if you think that Diamond is a positive person in your life then I can't tell you otherwise. Me and her now have an understanding, so all I can tell you is be careful."

"Jewel, I know that you two have a past," she said turning to face him, "but after having Chase, my ability to hate anyone and hold these long-ass grudges died. He took that away from me, and I couldn't be more thankful. As great of a father as you are, imagine the conversation I have to have with my son about Brandon. I have no good things to say about that man other than he gave me the greatest gift anyone could have ever given me, and for that I will forever be grateful. I don't have the chance to make things right with him, but you and Diamond do. Stop being so selfish and put all your personal feelings aside for your son. Take advantage, Jewel."

Deep down, he knew that she was right, but until Diamond let go of her hopes of them being together again, he didn't see how it could work.

"I hear you, but the best thing for me is to not be around her right now."

"I can't force you, Jewel," she said kissing him on the cheek, "I'll see you later tonight."

"Ay, I need you to do me a favor."

"What?" she asked turning back around.

"I need you to take the day off."

"What?"

"My mom is in town, and we're having dinner tonight."

"Jewel, it would have been nice if you would've told me before the day of."

"You weren't talking to me, remember?"

35

"Don't be petty. This is something important, but I can't just bail on work. We have full classes today."

"Baby, you're the boss. You can get out of whatever you want to get out of."

Reagan knew Jewel needed her by his side, and there was no way she wasn't going to be there. "Let me make a few calls," she said walking out of the room.

Twenty minutes later, she came back and said, "I'm all yours" as she flopped down on the bed.

"Thank you, baby," Jewel said kissing her on the lips, "This really means a lot to me."

"I know, babe," she said stroking his hand, "So what your mom say?"

"What, when I talked to her?"

"Yeah."

"Not too much. She said that she was in New York, but she really wanted us to talk or whatever."

"You told her about Joe?"

"Yeah, I could tell that she was hesitant at first, but I feel like whatever she has to say now, she can say in front of him and vice versa. I'm just ready to get this shit over with."

"Where is it?"

"Seasons 52 off Arden. My mom booked one of the dining rooms there."

"Fancy."

"I guess," Jewel said rolling his eyes.

$$$$$

A few hours later, he had managed to get everyone dressed and out of the house on time. He was beyond nervous. This was the first time in years that he and his mother and father had all been together in the same room, but this time was different. Jewel wasn't a helpless little boy anymore who had been completely sheltered from the world. He had become a man before he even really knew what one was. The streets raised him, gave him a home and love at times, and that's all he had ever known. He was a product of his environment, a manifestation of his parents' mistakes, and he was ready to face that.

"Before I forget," he said helping Chase into his car seat, "Isabella is throwing Gabby a baby shower Sunday, but she doesn't know about it yet."

"I'm really happy for her and K-2," Reagan said leaning back in her seat, "I mean they're young, but you can tell that they really love each other."

"Yeah, I can't lie, when I first met K-2, I couldn't stand his ass. Who would have thought that he would be marrying into a family I didn't even know I had and giving life to my first niece? Life is crazy, blood."

"I'ma have to call Ms. Izzy and see if she needs help with anything."

Deep down, Reagan envied the relationship K-2 and Gabrielle had. She couldn't help but to think back to her own pregnancy. Even though she loved her son, she wished there would have been some way for her to go back and do things differently, but reality always seemed to come and slap her in the face. Having a baby without the father present was not how she imagined her life going. It was hard at first, but Jewel became the prefect father to Chase. He embraced him as his own from the moment he was born.

Thirty minutes later, Jewel found himself in front of Seasons 52. His hands began to sweat as he circled the lot looking for a parking space. After finding a spot, he turned off the ignition and just sat there.

"I'm starving," Jailen said flying out of the car.

"J, wait," Reagan hurried to say as she unstrapped Chase from his car seat, but Jewel still remained seated. "Hey, babe, you ready?"

"Yeah," he said coming back from his thoughts. He hated how he felt like he had created this wall for so many years only to have his parents come and tear it down. He felt exposed. Reagan grabbed his hand as they and the kids walked inside towards the hostess' booth.

"Hi, welcome to Seasons 52. Do you have a reservation this evening?"

"Ummm, yeah, it should be under Laura Sanchez."

The upbeat, brown-skinned girl scrolled through her clipboard of names but couldn't find a *Sanchez* on the list. "Sorry, I don't have a Laura Sanchez. How many was the reservation for?"

"Nine, I believe."

"Okay, so we have a reservation for nine at 8:00 p.m. for a Laura Smith?"

"Yes, Smith, sorry, she's using her maiden name again."

"Oh, no problem, it happens all the time believe it or not. I'm Ayesha by the way. I'll be escorting you all to the Sonoma room. I think you are the first guests to arrive. Just have a seat wherever you like, and your waiter will be right out," she said walking them to their table.

"This is really nice," Reagan said admiring the restaurant's décor as she set Chase down to run around, "I wonder where everybody else is?"

"You know how niggas are," Jewel said shaking his head. He checked his phone, but he had no missed calls.

"We're here a little early," she said sitting down, "You want a drink or something?"

"Naw, I'm good."

Fifteen minutes later, K-2 and Gabrielle came strolling in. "Dad's still not here yet?" she asked scanning the room, "He left before we did, and he lives out here."

"Hey, Gabby," Reagan said getting up to give her a hug, "I swear you are all belly, girl."

"That's what I keep hearing, but I feel like a whale."

"A cute whale," K-2 said pinching her cheek.

"How far along are you now?"

"My due date is in a few weeks, but I feel like I'ma pop any day now," she smiled before sitting down next to Jewel, "So what's all this about exactly?"

"My mom said that she needed to have a conversation with me, so I figured that Joe and Isabella should be here too. Why should I have to suffer alone? A lot of shit transpired because of these three individuals."

"I feel you, bruh," K-2 said grabbing a piece of bread, "Battle to the death in this mothafucka."

"Keith, shut your messy-ass up," Gabrielle said smacking her lips.

"Naw, nothing like that. We're all adults, and plus, I have my sons here. Gabby's pregnant; there's no need for the drama. I guess I'm just looking for some answers, you know?"

"Well, whatever I can do to help, I'm here," she said rubbing the top of his hand when suddenly the doors opened again, and in walked Joe and Isabella.

"Sorry, we're late, guys."

"You were supposed to have been here," Gabrielle said getting up to give her dad a hug.

"Jewel, honestly, I was having second thoughts, man."

"Well, thank you for coming through," he said giving him a hug, "It really means a lot."

"Now that we're all here, where's the guest of honor?" Isabella slurred. She had a few drinks before they arrived. After all these years, she was more than comfortable with her relationship with Joe. They had built a beautiful family together, and she knew nothing could take that away, but despite it all, Laura still made her skin crawl.

"I don't know, but I'm starving," Joe said sitting down after giving both Chase and Jailen a kiss on the head. Just as the words left his lips, their waiter walked in carrying a cold metal pitcher of water filled to the brim with apple and ginger slices.

"Hello, I'm Matt, and I will be your server this evening. Ms. Smith has asked that I let you know that she's running a bit late, but feel free to begin eating as everything has already been taken care of," he said walking around the table filling each of their glasses.

"Well, in that case, let me get the Duck Wing 'Lollipops', the grilled chicken, the Shrimp Scampi Skillet, and the Crab and Spinach Stuffed Mushrooms," K-2 said looking down at the menu, "What you want, babe?"

"You are so greedy," Gabrielle said laughing, "I don't need an app. I'm ready to order."

"Okay, what can I get you?"

"Can I have the Shrimp Cavatappi Pasta, but can I add the branzino?"

"Sure."

"And you, sir?" he asked turning to Joe.

"Double the order on the appetizers, but can I add the Shishito Peppers and the Tuna Tartar?"

"The boys aren't gonna eat all that," Reagan said looking down at the menu, "Can I get another order of the grilled chicken and two of the Salumi Piccante pizzas?

"No problem. Anything to drink?" the waiter asked.

"No, not right now," Jewel said handing him the menus. Already he had lost his appetite.

An hour later while everyone feasted on surf and turf, Laura was still nowhere to be found.

"Maybe she got nervous," Gabrielle whispered noticing Jewel's anxious movements.

"Naw, she doesn't get nervous, believe me."

"Can I get anyone anything else to drink? Dessert?" the waiter asked coming in with his water pitcher again.

"No, that will be all," Laura said walking into the room.

"So nice of you to join us almost two hours later," Joe said looking down at his watch.

"Well, I thought I was being considerate by not being here. I figured why not enjoy your meal first before we get down to business," she said walking over to Jewel and placing a soft kiss on top of his head, "Isabelle, nice to see you again I suppose."

"It's Isabella."

"Does it really matter, sweetheart? And you are?" she asked stopping in front of Gabrielle.

"I'm Gabby," she said looking her up and down, "I'm Joe's daughter."

"You're a pretty little thing, aren't you? And you?" she asked motioning towards K-2.

"I'm Keith Tu, ma'am. I'm a friend of Jewel's."

"Nice to meet you," she smiled, "Jewel, are these your children?" Laura made her way to the end of the table in awe of her son's creations.

"Mom, this is Reagan, my wife, and this is my oldest son Jailen and our son Chase."

"Nice to meet you all," she said giving each one of them a hug, "Do you know who I am?"

Jailen shook his head no. "Dad, who is she?"

"J, this is my mother Laura. She's your grandma."

"Oh, like Grandma Paula or Grandma Izzy?"

"So first you wanted to play mama to my son, and now, you call yourself playing grandma to his?" Laura asked rolling her eyes.

"Playing?" Gabrielle asked struggling to stand up, "Who's playing? In just this short amount of time, she has been more of a mother to Jewel than you've ever been."

"Yeah, you're definitely that bitch's daughter," she said laughing as she sat down and crossed her legs. Her all white Chanel pants suit and the diamonds that covered her ear, neck, hands, and wrist glittered under the dim lighting.

"Yo, chill," Jewel said finally standing up, "Mom, you asked to talk to me, so talk."

"I've never been one for theatrics, but Jewel requested that you all be here for some god-awful reason, so here we are," she said turning her chair to face him, "Son, I know that on the outside, it appears that I have been some sort of absentee mother, and on one hand, I will agree to that, but on the other, it couldn't be further from the truth. As you may or may not remember, your father's career kept him very much occupied, and soon, so much so that he started the little family you see sitting before you today. I know that Joe loves you. You're his only son, but after Isabelle there got ahold of his balls, he lost everything that made him him unfortunately, and that didn't sit too well with our martial arrangement, so I had no other option."

"Then to what?" Jewel asked resting on her every last word. She was the missing piece of the puzzle that would finally allow him to leave his past in the past.

"Then to leave you in the care of your uncle," she smiled.

"Laura, don't do this," Joe said throwing his napkin on the table, "Jewel is a good boy. He got tangled in this bullshit you call life, but he's made a lot of changes for the better. Leave him alone."

"Mom, what are you talking about? I don't have any uncles," he said more confused than when he arrived.

"Laura, I'm begging you, don't do this," Joe said getting angry. He felt like the streets finally let his son go, but he knew Jewel wouldn't be safe from the life as long as she was around.

"Dad, I got this," he said refocusing his attention back on Laura, "What uncle?"

"My brother is, or I guess I should say was," she said looking down at the floor, "Maurice 'Golden' Smith."

Jewel felt as if the room was spinning and all the air escaped him. It was hard to catch his breath. "But...but..."

"I know that it must come as a shock, baby, but Golden was your uncle. Please don't be mad at him. I asked him not to say anything."

"But why?"

"Because she's a sleaze bag," Isabella finally said unable to take anymore, "Laura used Joe to help get her delinquent family members off when she was as guilty of their crimes as they were. Tell him."

"Your father and I were put together for the betterment of both the Sanchez and the Smith families, yes, but Joe always had his own agenda. How could I be married to a sympathizer? Once he became a prosecutor, I couldn't stand the sight of him, so thank you for taking this pathetic rat off my hands."

"Wait, none of this makes sense," Jewel said shaking his head.

"Once I found out where you hanging, I made it a point to have Golden look out for you, and I guess the rest is history."

Jewel couldn't deny that he had always felt a connection to him, but he could have never imagined how strong it really was.

"The dope game has been a part of our family for generations now, but Goldie chose the lower level. I always thought it was beneath him, but he wanted to be the grass roots one in the family. I guess that's where you get your tenacity from, but this path was never what I imagined for you, Jewel. I hoped that one day, you would be in a position to take my place, so I could be floating on an island somewhere."

"Like you don't do that already," Isabella said.

"Jealous? I know all that pro bono work ain't bringing in the checks like they used to," Laura laughed.

"I think it's time for us to go," Joe said grabbing Isabella's hand. Gabrielle and K-2 followed their lead as his mouth continued to hang open is disbelief.

"Jewel, I think me and the kids are gonna go wait in the car," Reagan said not knowing what else to say, "It was very nice meeting you, Ms. Smith."

"You as well, Reagan, and please, call me Laura. I hope I will be seeing you guys more often."

She just smiled as she placed a sleepy Chase against her chest and held Jailen's hand as they walked back to the car.

"What the fuck am I supposed to do with this? You're telling me that for over ten years, the man who I looked up to and idolized was actually my blood?"

"Jewel, with your father no longer in the picture, I wanted you to get that structure from somewhere. You were so delicate back then. I didn't know how you would have handled it along with the divorce and everything else. I needed to toughen you up, baby, and that silver spoon life wasn't going to cut it. These streets would have eaten you alive otherwise. I had to take away everything to build you into the man you were supposed to be."

"I don't know what you want me to say."

"I know that this is a lot to take in right now, but after finding out that Joe had resurfaced, I thought that it was time for you to know the truth especially with Golden gone. May he rest in peace, but, baby, you have family who would love to finally meet you."

"I don't know," he said getting up from the table, "I'm sorry. I gotta go."

"Just think about what I said, okay?" Laura said as he left without looking back, "I'll be here."

Chapter 5

The next day, Jewel was up before the sun was. He spent all night thinking about the conversation he had with Laura. He still didn't know how to process it, but he was tired of being in a state of confusion. He knew that Reagan was going to try and help him get through it, but he just needed space. With Sacario and his family coming over, Jewel planned to get just that, so he spent the morning preparing for their arrival. He rented a bouncy house and a snow cone machine for the kids. This was the first time all of their families had been together before since the wedding, and he wanted to make it special.

"Jewel?" Reagan asked from the top of the stairs as she wiped the mid-morning sleep from her eyes, "Jewel?"

"Yeah," he said coming from the backyard.

"The doorbell's ringing."

"My bad, babe, I was tryna let the party guy in through the back, but the chain on the gate got stuck."

"Party guy?"

"Give me two seconds," he said running back outside.

Reagan walked into their room and threw on a pair of shorts and a small white tee before she headed downstairs.

"What is all this?" she said to herself noticing all of the black and white balloons and streamers that filled each room, "Jewel?"

"Yeah, the gate should be unlocked now," she heard him say, "Let me know if you need anything else."

"Jewel?"

"Yes, babe," he said closing the door behind him.

"What is all this?"

"It's for today."

"Today? What's today?"

"I think I forgot to tell you with everything that was going on, but Sacario and his fam are about to slide through, so I got a few things for the kids."

"That's nice and all, but don't you think we need to actually talk about what happened last night?"

"Nope," he said smiling, "Today, I just want to relax and kick back with my peoples. No drama. I know I'ma have to address this shit with my mom eventually, but just not today, okay?"

"Okay, baby," she said grabbing his face and placing a soft kiss on his lips, "What do you need help with?"

"The caterer should be here in like the next hour. Can you clear off the counters in the kitchen for me?"

"Yeah, let me just go change my clothes," Reagan said wanting to get ready for the day. As she ran up the stairs, she could hear her phone ring. From the tone, she already knew who was on the other end, so she tried to catch it before Jewel noticed.

"Hey, girl," she said closing the door.

"Hey, you at work?"

"No, I took yesterday and today off."

"You never take days off," Diamond said laughing, "What's the special occasion?"

"Jewel's mom came into town."

"What?"

"Yes, girl, she showed up at the wedding but ended up leaving before it was over. Before she did though, she gave Joe her number to give to Jewel. He calls her, and we all had dinner last night."

"All? Who is all?"

"It was me, Jewel, and the boys. Gabby and K-2 came, and Joe and his wife, and then Jewel's mom came like right after we all finished eating."

"How'd he take it?"

"He was hella nervous of course, but then the shit hit the fan last night, and now today, this nigga is up early morning having balloons, streamers, and bounce houses put up."

"For what?"

"I guess some of his friends are coming out from the Bay, so you know he's doing whatever he can to distract himself."

"He's so bad at dealing with shit I swear. He's always been like that though."

"It's only getting worse."

"Well, I was gonna come and get Jailen today, but I guess I'll let him stay if ya'll are doing something."

"Why don't you come over?"

"I don't know about all that. Jewel made it more than clear about how he feels about me, and I'm really not in the mood for his antics."

"Just think about it, okay?"

"Ok, I'll hit you back later. Kiss my baby for me," Diamond said before hanging up.

$$$$$

A Few Hours Later...

"You got everything?" Sacario asked his daughter as he unbuckled her out of her booster seat.

"Yep," she said looking around the quiet neighborhood, "Where are we, Daddy?"

"We're at my friend Jewel's house."

"Is it his birthday or something?"

"No, we're just gonna hang out for a little bit," he said holding her hand as he led her up the small flight of steps, "You got my baby acting like she ain't never been nowhere before."

"Sorry, I don't have our 4-year old daughter around a bunch of thug-ass niggas," Kiko said.

"Here you go." All Sacario could do was shake his head. "Please try and act like you're having a good time."

"I'll try," she smiled as he rang the doorbell.

"Hi," Reagan said hurrying to answer, "How are you guys?"

"Hey, Rea, we're good. You remember my wife Kiko, right?"

"Of course, so nice to see you again. I'm surprised he doesn't bring you around more often."

"Don't mind her. She's a little anti-social."

"Girl, me too," Reagan said laughing, "Don't worry about it. Come on, Jewel's in the back."

"What's all this?" Sacario asked noticing all of the decorations and food in the kitchen.

"Well, Jewel wanted to do something nice since you guys were coming out here. He got a bouncy house for the kids, hella food, a..."

"I swear this nigga can't ever just let me do anything."

"What you mean?" Reagan asked grabbing a sandwich from off one of the platters that sat on the counter.

"Man, I wasn't trying to say anything until tonight, but the whole reason for us coming out here was because I wanted to throw ya'll an official wedding party. I rented a party bus, I got us a section at Rain..."

"Rain?"

46

"Yeah, they switched owners and reopened it a few months ago. I wanted to treat my nigga to a night out, and now, he's trying to outdo me as usual."

"That's sweet, Sacario. Thank you. He really needs this, believe me."

"Why, what's up?"

"I think I'll let him tell you," she said walking towards the back, "Jewel, Sacario's here."

"What's up, bruh?" he asked coming inside the house a few seconds later, "Ya'll just got here?"

"Yeah, but, ay, what's all this about?"

"I thought I'd do it up for the kids today and what not. You hungry, mamas?" he asked bending down to talk to Arianna.

"Yes," she said shyly.

"There's more food outside."

"Kiko, can you go make her plate? I need to talk to Jewel for a sec."

"Yeah."

"I'll go out there with ya'll," Reagan said leading the way.

"You want a beer or something?" Jewel asked walking into the kitchen.

"What you got?"

"Some New Castles."

"Yeah, let me get one."

"So what's up? I thought your potnah was coming through?" Jewel asked walking over to the refrigerator.

"He is. He wanted to drive his own whip though. He should be here by now. He left a little after we did."

Ding. Dong. Ding. Dong. Ding. Dong.

"I'll be right back," Jewel said as he walked out of the kitchen.

"What's up, Chosen One?" K-2 said as he opened the door before he could reach it.

"Hey, you good?" Gabrielle asked giving Jewel a hug.

"Yeah, I'm straight. Sacario's in the kitchen."

"You tell him yet?"

"Tell me what?" he asked walking towards the door.

"Where are the boys?" Gabrielle could feel the tension in the air, so she used it as a distraction.

"Sleep still I think."

"I'll go get them ready," she said heading up the stairs.

"Yo, what's up?" Sacario asked looking between K-2 and Jewel, "Somebody say something."

"So you know how I was supposed to be meeting up with my mom, right?" Jewel walked into the living room and sat down.

"Yeah."

"Well, we had dinner last night."

"K told me they were coming up yesterday for that. How'd it go?"

"This nigga here, blood, has been blessed," K-2 said unable to contain his excitement.

"To make a long story short, my mom told me that Golden is really my uncle," Jewel said looking down on the floor.

"What?" Sacario asked leaning back against the couch.

"You should have seen my face," K-2 said laughing, "Everybody always knew that G favored Jewel, but now we know why."

"So that's your mom's brother?"

"Blood brother," K-2 chimed in again.

"That's crazy that all that time he never said anything. I wonder if he knew."

"Oh, he knew."

"Basically once my mom found out where I was hanging out, she put it in Golden's ear to look after me. She said I was too soft because we had always been so well off, and she wanted the streets to toughen me up."

"Ay, yo, moms sounds like an OG."

"You have no idea, blood. This nigga Jewel has the keys to the kingdom now. It's just a matter of what he's gonna do with them."

"What are you gonna do?" Sacario asked in all seriousness. He knew how close Jewel and Golden were. He had trained him how to be a soldier in the streets, but Jewel turned his back on everything he grew to know. The M.A.C. Boys wasn't the same without him, and now that Sacario knew that the clique ran through his veins, he was determined to pull the team back together.

Ding. Dong. Ding. Dong. Ding. Dong.

"Hold that thought," Jewel said getting up. *Saved by the mothafucking bell.* He hurried to open the door hoping not to have to discuss his family tree anymore.

"Can I help you?"

"Yeah, what's up with you? I'm Hassan. I'm looking for Sacario."

"Oh, ok, I'm Jewel," he said giving him dap, "Sacario and K-2 are inside. Come in."

"Thanks, bruh," Hassan said walking into the house.

"You want something to drink or anything?"

"Naw, I'm good. Right on though."

"There he is," K-2 said standing up as Jewel and Hassan entered the room, "What took you so long, nigga?"

"I had to bust a few moves, homie. I didn't know we were on a schedule," he said sitting down.

"Don't mind him," Sacario said getting up to greet his friend, "I think he needs to smoke or something."

"On that note," K-2 said pulling out an eighth from his pocket as he emptied the bright green buds on the coffee table in front of him.

"Blood, I swear you don't have no respect," Jewel said, "Use a magazine or something, nigga."

"My bad, bruh," he said sweeping the crumbs back together with his finger.

"Anyway, I know ya'll met already, but let me formally introduce you. Jewel, this is Hassan Williams. I've been knowing him since I was a young one, and Hassan, this is Jewel Sanchez, my M.A.C. brotha."

"It's good to finally put a face with the name," Hassan said.

"Likewise."

"So what I miss?"

"Well, I was just telling Jewel about our little situation," Sacario said knowing that he was done with the family talk at least for now.

"Fill me in, blood."

"These nigga from 23rd Street shot up K-2's storefront."

"For what?" Jewel asked scooting to the edge of his seat. Even though he wasn't affiliated anymore, he became even more protective over the few potnahs he still had left.

"Cause they were mad. It was on some retaliation shit I guess, but the coldest part is that I don't bang no more. All this shit was to send a message to Cari."

"What's been going on out there?"

"Shit is straight. I have everything under control," Sacario said sitting up," You know how these clown-ass niggas are, bruh."

"Yeah, I do know, so that's why I'm asking. How many people you got out there?"

"Enough."

"I mean if this is just an isolated incident then you're good, but if you're trying to push up on somebody's area or vice versa then shit is guaranteed to hit the fan. You know niggas don't fuck with the M.A.C. Boys."

"What would you do in this situation, blood?" K-2 asked as he lit the blunt. He had always looked up to Sacario, and he valued his leadership, but after finding out who Jewel really was, his respect for him grew even more than it had during the past year.

"I mean if it's just niggas being pussy then I would have some hitters beat they ass. Make sure you put that message out there that M.A.C. is not to be fucked with, but if it's about some work then I would put the pressure on them. That's the only way to expand. It might get ugly though, but you need room to move, feel me?" he said taking the tree from K-2. His chest burned as the smoke saturated his lungs, but with everything going on around him, he craved the nostalgic sensation.

"How much work you got?"

"I'm cool right now, but I mean we could always use some more. Smackz be tripping though. Ever since Golden died, God rest his soul, he has the trap locked down even more than before."

"Let me talk to him," Jewel said.

"Talk to who?" Reagan asked walking into the living room with Kiko and Gabrielle.

"His long-lost cousin," K-2 said laughing.

"Who?"

"We'll talk about it later, babe," Jewel said standing up, "What's up?"

"Sacario, you wanna tell him or should I?"

"Tell me what?"

"I'll tell him," he said smiling, "Bruh, after Pop's funeral, something in you changed, and I know you needed a breather. I can't say that the clique doesn't need you or even miss you, but we respect you wanting to settle down and really be the father that most of us never had. Over this past year, you welcomed a new little one into the world and married the woman of your dreams, but throughout this time, I think that you forgot about yourself in the process, so tonight, everything is on me. I rented a party bus, I booked a section at Rain…"

"And I agreed to babysit," Gabrielle said interrupting, "So you have no excuse not to go."

"Man," Jewel said unable to stop himself from smiling, "Ya'll know that's not my thing anymore."

"Well, for tonight it is. No drama just you enjoying yourself with those who love you," Reagan said wrapping her arms around his waist. She would do anything to get him to relax and be himself again.

"You knew about this?" he asked kissing her on top of her head.

"Barely," she said laughing, "but I haven't been out in years, so I'm all for it."

"Well, if wifey says yes then I guess that's the move for tonight."

"To Jewel and Reagan," K-2 said putting weed in the air.

"To Jewel and Reagan."

Chapter 6

"Everybody upstairs," Gabrielle said rounding up all the kids. Her big belly made it hard to see Chase and Arianna scurrying beneath her.

"Babe, you sure you don't want me to stay with you?" K-2 asked coming up from behind her.

"Keith, now you know that you do not want to stay here with all these kids," she said laughing, "Go and have fun."

"I just feel bad."

"Why? It's not like I can have my big-ass in the club pop, lock, and dropping it. The whole night sounds exhausting to me anyway. Go and get all this shit out of your system cause in a few weeks, you are gonna be on permanent daddy duty," she said kissing him on the cheek.

"Don't remind me," he said sighing.

"K," she yelled as she hit him in the chest.

"Damn," he said coughing a little, "You know I can't wait til my lil mama comes. I don't regret my decision, Gabrielle. Our family means everything to me. I'm here for the long run," he said looking into her eyes.

"I love you."

"I love you too."

"So we staying over here tonight or what?"

"Yeah, we might as well. I know it's gonna be hella late by the time ya'll get back anyway. We can just go see my parents tomorrow before we head back."

"That works for me." He was happy to know that his plan to surprise her was right on track.

Ever since she found out that she was pregnant, all she could focus on was her baby. Her young and reckless ways became apparent after she got shot, and Gabrielle didn't like who she let the world turn her into. Being in love with Pop exposed her to a world that she wasn't ready for, but that chase got her high. She couldn't see anything but their fabricated future together until she had to watch him be lowered into the cold ground. When he died, her infatuation with the streets died too, but in the beginning of her and K-2's relationship, she noticed that he shared the same traits she thought she used to love about Pop, and that scared her. She couldn't afford to make the same mistake twice.

"Auntie Gabby, I got the popcorn," Jailen said coming out of the kitchen.

"Okay, go upstairs and grab Chase. I'll get Ari."

"K," he said running up the stairs.

"I got her, babe," K-2 said picking up his niece. She had blue sugar painted along her mouth.

"Thank you."

"Where she get this candy from?" he asked trying to wipe it away.

"Me."

After agreeing to watch the kids, Gabrielle went to the store and got candy, popcorn, cookies, and had Jailen download as many Disney movies as he could.

"Don't be having these little niggas hopped up on hella sugar all night, blood."

"Not tonight, Keith," she said walking up the stairs, "Not tonight."

"Yo," Sacario yelled, "K, blood, what's up? You coming or what?"

"Yes, please take his ass somewhere, Sacario," Gabrielle said rolling her eyes, "He's getting on my goddamn nerves."

"Give me a second, bruh. I'm bout to go get Ari situated."

"Yep," he said walking back into the kitchen as Iamsu's "Backflip" blared through the speakers that were strung throughout the house.

"You want another one?" Reagan slurred a little as she filled everyone's shot glass with Patron, salt, and a cold lime wedge. This was her first time going out in a long time, and she was determined to enjoy herself.

"Naw, I'm good, sis. Those three double-shots got a nigga feeling lovely," he said sitting next to Kiko, "You want one, babe?"

"I'm good on the Patron, but I will take some of that Slurricane though," she said sliding her glass over to Reagan.

"Me too," Hassan said getting up, "It's sweet as fuck, but it'll get you there."

"Where's Jewel? He's missing the whole pregame," Sacario said taking a sip from Kiko's glass.

"Still upstairs getting ready," Reagan said, "You know how he is."

"And I thought I was a pretty nigga," K-2 said walking into the kitchen.

"What time is it, Sani?"

"Almost 10:00 p.m."

"Ay, yo, go tell that nigga to hurry up," Sacario said, "I mean this whole night is supposed to be about him."

"In the meantime, burn something," K-2 said sitting down.

"I got some swishers in the car," Hassan said, "Let me go grab them right quick."

"That should be some motivation for Jewel," Reagan said walking up the stairs as he walked outside.

Hassan ran over to his car when he saw an all-white Altima pull up behind him. He couldn't see who was inside, but he intended on finding out.

"Ay, you need to get in here?" he yelled.

"Naw, you're good," Diamond said sliding out. The tight white Maxi dress she wore hugged each and every curve she worked so hard to get back. Hassan tried not to stare, but he couldn't take his eyes off her.

"You a friend of Jewel and Reagan?" he asked stepping in front of her before her white and gold Giuseppe *Cruel Summer's* hit the first step.

"You could say that."

"I'm Hassan."

"Diamond," she said extending her crystal covered hand.

"Nice to meet you," he said finally moving out of the way.

"You too," she said before making her way inside.

"You made it," Reagan screamed as she ran into Diamond at the door, "I thought you were gonna flake."

"You drunk already?"

"I've been dranking, I've been dranking," she sang.

"Ok, ok, I need to get on your level, mama."

"Come on, everybody's in the kitchen," Reagan said as she began to walk away.

"Is Jewel in there?"

"No, he's still upstairs getting dressed. The bus is about to be here in like twenty minutes though."

"I'ma run up there and talk to him. After everything that happened, I don't feel right taking his check like that, so I wanna give it back. I just don't need the drama right now, you know?"

"Good luck with that, girl," Reagan said walking back into the kitchen to rejoin the party. She was honestly tired of all the drama between Jewel and Diamond. She just wanted to enjoy her night.

54

Counterfeit *Dreams* 4

Diamond took a deep breath before she headed up the stairs. She knew that more times than not, she lost her cool when it came to Jewel. Even though she wanted him to be happy, she hated that he couldn't be happy with her. For so long, she played the 'what-if' game when it came to him, but when they reconnected, she believed that he would be hers forever. Neither of them were perfect, and they both made mistakes when it came to their relationship, but if she wanted him to see that she had changed then she had to change.

Knock. Knock. Knock.

"Reagan, I told you give me like five minutes," he said opening the door with his shirt unbuttoned. Diamond tried not to look down at his hard body, but his creamy caramel skin distracted her. "Are you serious, blood? I thought we..."

"Listen, before you even start, let me first say that Reagan invited me."

"Of course she did."

"But I'm not here for the drama, Jewel. I just wanted to give you this," she said pulling the untouched check from out of her small, golden clutch, "Here."

"What's this for?"

"What do you mean what's it for? You threw a fucking blank check at me like I was a prostitute. No matter if you like me or don't like me, I will always be the mother of your son. The whole point of us going house hunting together was for our son, but if we're not coming together as a collective then I don't need your money, so here."

"Why is everything so difficult with you?"

"With me? You send mixed messages, Jewel, but I get it. Believe me, at this point, I get it," she said placing the check in his hand before walking back down the stairs.

$$$$$

"You find the swishers?" K-2 asked as Hassan entered the kitchen.

"Yeah, here," he said handing them to him.

"K, roll a few up for the bus too."

"Yep."

"Ay, who is lil baby in the all-white?" Hassan asked no one in particular.

"Who?" Sacario asked.

"Diamond?" Reagan's ears perked up. She didn't know if it was because of all of the tequila in her system, but she thought Hassan was fine. His milky chocolate skin, broad arms, and tattoo and diamond covered chest tempted her for just a second. She and Diamond rarely ever talked about other dudes other than Jewel, but she figured they obviously had the same taste.

"Diamond?" Sacario asked almost spitting out his drink, "Naw, bruh, that's not what you want."

"Don't do that," Reagan said.

"What's wrong with her?"

"For one, she's crazy as fuck," K-2 said sealing the blunt closed.

"Not only that, but she's Jewel's first baby mama."

"She's the mother of his oldest son," Reagan corrected him.

"Man, you know what I mean."

"Enough said."

"I'ma hook something up," Reagan offered.

"Naw, lil mama, it's good. There's already too many strings attached for a nigga like me. Thank you though," Hassan said trying to save face. He didn't want anyone to see his disappointment, but he lived by a code. Being that Jewel and Sacario were like blood, he couldn't imagine crossing that line no matter how much he wanted to. It was all about respect.

"So you kick it with your nigga's BM?" Kiko asked finally interested in the night's festivities.

"Yeah, I mean everything hasn't always been good between us, but I think we're in a cool spot now," she said for the hundredth time

"Girl, you better than me. I couldn't do no shit like that. I would be thinking the whole time that she would be trying to fuck my man."

"It's not like that..."

"Hey, guys, I think the bus just pulled up," Diamond said walking into the kitchen.

"Speaking of the devil," K-2 said tucking the blunts back into the box.

"Huh?"

"The bus."

"Oh."

"Diamond, these are Jewel's friends Sacario and K-2, and Sacario's wife Kiko."

"Hi, nice to meet you," Kiko waved.

"Hi."

"And this is Sacario's potnah Hassan. I think you already met," Reagan said bumping her a little.

"Yeah, outside. Nice to see you again," she smiled. Hassan just melted.

"Alright, now that everybody is up to speed, let's get this show on the road," Sacario said making sure he had everything he needed before he grabbed Kiko's hand.

"Gabrielle," K-2 yelled from the bottom of the stairs, "Gabrielle."

"Why would you be yelling like that?" she asked flying out of Jailen's room with a bright pink scarf wrapped around her head, "Are you fucking stupid? I just got Chase to lay down, and you know his bad-ass never wants to lay down. No offense, Rea."

"None taken," she laughed, "I know my baby."

"I just wanted to say, 'bye.'"

"Bye, I'll see ya'll when you get back," she said walking back into the room. Her hormones had her all over the place.

"She talking about Chase is sleep. Her ass was in there sleep," he said walking outside, "I just like fucking with her."

Jewel came downstairs as everyone was boarding the bus. He was having second thoughts about going especially with Diamond in attendance, but he knew he needed the room to breathe. His everyday life was slowly suffocating him, and as much as he loved his family, he couldn't imagine spending another night at home.

"You ready, babe?"

"Yep," he said wanting to get into the spirit of the night.

As they walked outside, the coldish air soothed Jewel. He wanted to make the best of the night, but he didn't feel like he really deserved to enjoy himself. He wasn't going to let Reagan know that though.

"About time, nigga," Sacario said standing up as he entered the bus, "You acting like you not tryna fuck with it or something."

"My bad, blood, it's not that. I appreciate this, bruh, forreal. I haven't been out in bleams."

"Then what is it then?" Sacario asked over the music that echoed around them.

"Man, fuck all this talking shit. Turn up, my nigga," K-2 said handing Jewel a shot of Ciroc.

Without second guessing himself, he threw the cold fiery liquid down his throat and growled as the burning sensation consumed him.

"That's my boy," Sacario said getting hyped again, "Ay, Diamond, tell the driver to turn it up."

"K," she said getting up.

"Rain about to be lit tonight," K-2 said.

"Rain?" Jewel asked barely able to even hear himself think.

"Huh?" Sacario asked.

"Nothing," he said filling his glass again. It was crazy to him how life came back full circle. He still remembered the night he and Brandon first met Reagan and Robyn. He knew that there was something special about her then, but he never would've guessed that four years later she would be his wife. The road for them from day one was never easy, but despite it all, they made it through. He just wished he could say the same thing about Pop. He missed his brother, and being in the position where he lost and gained everything all at the same time was too much too bear, but he didn't have a choice. There was no turning back.

$$$$$

Feeling himself, Hassan became bored with the night's activities. Even though he knew she was off limits, he couldn't keep his eyes off Diamond. He watched as she sat with Reagan pretending to drink as much as she was while watching Jewel like it was her job. He didn't have any kids of his own, but he knew how the game usually went, and from the look in her eyes, she wasn't over Jewel, but he loved a challenge.

"You having fun?" he asked walking up to the front and sitting in front of her and Reagan.

"The night hasn't even began," Reagan said swinging her glass as the bus hit a bump in the road. Cranberry juice and vodka covered her and the floor.

"Jewel," she said whining as she walked to the back where he, Sacario, and K-2 were.

"I'll take that as a yes," Hassan said laughing, "What about you, Ms. Lady?"

"It's cool," she yelled.

"You and Reagan really close?"

"Yeah, something like that," Diamond said fidgeting a little.

"Naw, that's what up. I mean I don't know too many women who kick it with their child's father and wife like that. Like on some sister-wife shit or something."

"I'm different I guess," she said becoming irritated. She hated how no matter what, Reagan and Jewel's relationship was constantly thrown in her face, but she didn't know how to stay away.

"No offense though. I think it's admirable that you're able to be a team player, feel me?"

"What's that supposed to mean?" Diamond asked snapping her neck.

"That you still feeling the nigga. I mean a blind mothafucka could see that."

"First off, Hassan, was it? You don't know me, and from the looks of it, you must not know my baby daddy much, or you wouldn't be all up in my face like this."

"Is that right?"

"Yeah, that's right, and it looks like you got a couple dollars," she said flicking his gold chain, "so why don't you go buy your ass some business?"

"You always this mean?"

"Always," she said clinching her clutch as she stood up and walked to the back to find Reagan.

I want her, he thought as he watched her sashay away.

Fifteen minutes later, the bus pulled up right in front of Rain. The alcohol Jewel had been drowning himself with was finally numbing every feeling he had, and for the first time in a long time, he felt like he could breathe again. The weight of the world had been lifted from his shoulders for just one night, and he wanted to enjoy every minute of it.

"Ya'll have a good night," the driver said opening the doors, "I'll be back here at 3:30 a.m. sharp."

"Good looking, sir," Sacario said handing him a crisp $100 bill as he grabbed Kiko's hand helping her navigate through the crowd. The line was wrapped around the block.

Once the city heard that club Rain was reopening their doors, the club had been packed for weeks. Sacario was happy with the turn out. He knew Jewel would be hesitant at first, but he was determined to get him out of his funk and finally reunite with the M.A.C. Boys again. Truth be told, he didn't want to do it all on his own.

"Ay, I'm looking for Lamont," he said walking up to the bouncer who headed the line.

"He's already expecting you, my man. Ya'll go right in."

"Thanks," Sacario said making sure Kiko stayed right beside him. With her mocha skin, tight black jeans, six-inch heels, and slanted eyes, he didn't feel like having to beat a nigga's ass before the end of the night. When he looked back, K-2 was right behind Kiko next to Jewel and Reagan while Diamond and Hassan trailed the back. He was amused by the expression on Diamond's face. She was mad at the world.

Why did she even come? he thought feeling bad for his boy.

When they walked inside, it was like stepping back in time. Everything was exactly as they all remembered it.

"Turn up," K-2 said bouncing through the crowd. Even though he was 21, he didn't experience the club life much especially with Gabrielle around, so he intended on taking full advantage of his freedom for the night.

"Ay, our section is over here," Sacario said walking to the back.

"Jewel, I gotta go to the bathroom. I'll meet you guys there," Reagan said grabbing Diamond's hand.

Kiko stood off to the side with her arms folded and her eyes glued to her phone. Sacario bumped her almost knocking it out of her hand.

"What?" she snapped.

"Man, don't be like this tonight. You've been hella anti-social this whole fucking time. You've barely even said two words."

"I don't know these bitches," she said rolling her eyes.

"Kiko," he said motioning toward the bathroom.

"Wow, you know what? All of a sudden, I have the urge to pee in front of a room full of strangers. Yay! Look at me being all social and what not," she said before following Reagan and Diamond's path as she rolled her eyes.

The line spilled out into the hallway, but she cut in front of the mob of drunken girls who one-by-one came in and out. She just wanted to hurry up and find her unwanted, new best friends.

"Hey, there you are," Reagan said washing her hands as Kiko trekked through the beige paper towel covered floor, "I've been looking everywhere for you."

"Sorry, I was out there with Sacario, but I'm here now," she said forcing a smile.

"You're not having fun, huh?" Reagan asked trying not to slip on the small puddles of water beneath her.

"Why you say that?" Kiko hoped she wasn't being too obvious.

"You're just so quiet. I feel like I don't know anything about you other than that you're married to Sacario, and you have a 4-year old daughter."

"You know what? You're right. I'm sorry. I don't have much luck when it comes to other females to be honest. I really just hang around my family and my best friend who is more like my sister, so I'm not really good with situations like these."

"No, I get it. I mean I'm really just around my kids and Jewel."

"How'd you and Diamond link up?" Kiko asked wanting to finally get the details on their situation.

"I know that a lot of people still don't get it," Reagan started as Diamond made her way out of the stall over to the sink, "but me and Jewel got together a few years ago, and we had a really rocky relationship in the beginning."

"If that's what you wanna call it," she said washing her hands.

"When we broke up, somehow, Diamond and Jewel ran into each other, and surprise, there she is with his 8-year old son."

"It was fate," she smiled.

"They went through whatever they went through, and me and her for sure went through a lot, but we're like one big, happy family, or some shit now."

"Or some shit."

"Sacario doesn't talk about stuff like this, so no offense. I wasn't tryna get all in ya'll business or anything."

Diamond just smiled.

"Well, I know how much Sacario means to Jewel especially now, so you might be stuck with us," Reagan said hanging all over Kiko.

"How much did she have?" she whispered to Diamond.

"Too much." She couldn't help but roll her eyes.

When they walked back out into the club, they saw Jewel, Sacario, K-2, and Hassan already filling their glasses to the brim with D'usse.

"I guess it's one of them nights," Reagan said walking up and grabbing a glass for herself.

"Rea, I think you're good, babe. Why don't you just chill? We didn't get this booth for nothing."

"Jewel, you're not my daddy," she said snatching the glass back from him, "Like you wanna enjoy your night, I wanna enjoy mine too."

"Yeah, a little too much," he said becoming irritated.

"Don't do me in front of all these people, Jewel. I'm grown," she said walking off.

"I'll go get her," Diamond offered before following behind Reagan as she made her way to the bar.

"Yo, what the fuck was that about?"

"Who knows," Jewel said not having the energy to try and read her mind, "Man, where's the weed at?"

"Right here, my brotha," K-2 said lighting another blunt allowing him to escape.

$$$$$

Thirty minutes later, Diamond came back, but Reagan was nowhere to be found.

"Please don't tell me you lost my girl?" Jewel asked standing up.

"First off, your bitch is passed out locked in the bathroom. I tried to get her to keep talking, but she's over. I think you need to go get her."

Without having to be told twice, he made his way through the crowd of people who flooded the dance floor to get to the women's bathroom.

"Reagan?" he asked poking his head inside, "Rea?"

"Ummmmmm, nigga, do you know where you at?" a girl asked as she stood against the wall.

"Ay, lil baby, calm down. My girl is in here."

"And?"

"And maybe you should mind your own business," he said pushing the door open and walking inside, "Reagan?"

"Jewel?" he heard her voice faintly flow through the stall.

"Babe, open the door."

"Jewel, I don't feel good."

"I bet. You drank like you was one of my potnahs or something. You don't weigh that much, Rea. Your body doesn't need all that."

"No, not because of that, but because of this."

"What?"

"This place," she slurred, "Jewel, do you realize where we are? I almost died in this place. Pop...and Brandon. So much destruction surrounded us, and I'm responsible for most of it. I know Brandon is dead because of me. I could've ended it after the first time it happened, but no, I wanted to see how far I could string him along," she said beginning to cry.

"Rea, let's not do this here, okay? We can talk more at home. Can you please open the door?" he asked jiggling the door handle.

"It's all my fault. I have to look my son in the eye one day and tell him that his father is dead because of me."

"Rea, please open the door," he said again as he noticed a small crowd forming behind him as they waited to hear more of her secret confessions.

"I look at you, and I know that losing Pop is something that you never recovered from. Shit, even losing Brandon, but after Golden, I could see the light in you dim so much that it was barely even there anymore. It scares me because I see so much of myself in you. The pain, the regret, all of it is like looking in a mirror, but I put on this bright and pretty face every day because I'm so afraid of how the world will look at me if I don't. Brandon did a lot of bad things to a lot of bad people, but it crushes me that he didn't get to see Chase's first steps or his first tooth come in."

"Would you have really wanted him to?" Jewel asked leaning against the stall door.

"I don't know. My choice has been made for me, so I guess it doesn't really matter."

"Reagan, you can't keep blaming yourself. You had nothing to do with any of that shit, so stop it. Now, open the door."

"I think I'ma throw up," she said standing up.

Jewel could hear the clinks of the bottoms of her heels hitting the porcelain tile.

"Baby, I'm bout to go get a cab, so we can go home, okay? Don't move. I'll be right back."

Reagan couldn't utter a word as the alcohol that filled her stomach continued to splash into the toilet as Jewel went to say his goodbyes.

Chapter 7

"K, it's only 9 a.m. It's not like you have to be at the shop today. Why are we up so early?" Gabrielle whined as she rolled out of bed.

"Look, your mom called me and said that her and Joe wanted to have everybody over for breakfast or whatever before we left, so you can call her back and tell her your ass wanna stay sleep."

"Fine," she said with an attitude as she got up, grabbed her stuff, and headed for the bathroom.

"One down, ten more niggas to go," he said walking out of the guestroom trying not to wake the kids who were still sleep on pallets covering the floor.

Gabrielle's mother Isabella put K-2 in charge of making sure she got to the baby shower on time, but after last night, he doubted if anybody would be up before the sun went down.

"Kiko," he said banging on the door down the hall, "Kiko, Kiko, Kiko, Kiko."

"Bruh, what the fuck is wrong with you?" Sacario asked snatching the door open.

"Ay, I need ya'll dressed in like forty-five minutes. Isabella's setting up now."

"Alright, blood," he said grabbing his head.

"K, we're up. We're up," she groaned.

"Don't play with me, Kiko. Get up and don't say anything to Gabby when you see her. Brunch, breakfast, that's it."

"I haven't said shit yet, have I?"

"Let's keep it like that," K-2 said heading for the stairs.

"I heard you," Hassan said walking past him to the bathroom.

"My man." He ran up the stairs, and as he approached Jewel's room, he noticed the door was slightly cracked open. "Ay…"

"I'm up. Joe just called," he said yawning.

"Alright, cool, I say we leave in like the next hour."

"Yep," Jewel said getting out of bed, "Rea?" He walked over to the other side searching for her face, but it was hard to tell where she was as she laid wrapped up underneath the covers.

"Yeah," she managed to say.

"You need anything?"

"Can you get me something to drink please?"

"Yeah."

He ran downstairs and grabbed her a small glass of ice water. "Here," he said handing it to her once he got back inside the room as she unraveled herself.

"What happened last night?" she asked pulling her hair up into a bun once she came up for air.

"Man," Jewel said shaking his head, "We don't even need to talk about that."

"Was it that bad?"

"You was just in your feelings. It was probably cause of all that Patron and Ciroc you was throwing back."

"Naw, I think it was because of that pill I popped."

"What pill?"

Jewel knew that Reagan wanted to have a good time, but popping x wasn't even her style.

"Diamond gave me an e-pill on the bus, so I was like..."

"Why would you pop pills with her? How does that even sound?"

"Jewel, don't start."

"You just act different when you get around her. It's like you're trying to impress her or something." "Impress her for what?" Reagan asked finally sitting up.

"That's what I'm still trying to figure out."

"Me and Diamond..."

"You and Diamond, what? There shouldn't even be a you and Diamond. She is not your friend, and I promise you one day, she is going to prove that. I know that you feel guilty about what happened to Robyn, but you can't just replace her, and I don't even know why you would want to. To be honest, Robyn wasn't shit. If you forgot, she was the reason you got your ass beat on multiple occasions. You need to do a better job at picking your potnahs, Rea."

"It was complicated," she said putting her head down.

"Surround yourself with people who actually give a fuck about you and not just the ones who pretend to," Jewel said walking into the bathroom and closing the door behind him.

$$$$$

An hour later, everyone met by the front door ready to get the festivities started.

"Where we going, Dad?" Jailen asked as they walked outside to the car.

"To Grandpa and Grandma Izzy's house to have breakfast."

"You think they made pancakes?" he asked.

"That's probably all they made for you," Gabrielle said laughing.

"Alright, one, two, three, four," K-2 counted off, "five, six, seven, eight, nine. Okay, I think that's everybody."

"Why are you being so extra today?" she asked pinching his cheek, "You act like we've never ate over there before."

"I'm just hungry I guess."

"It's probably cause of all that drank last night."

"Maybe. I was turnt up to the max though," he said dancing in a circle around her.

"Let me find out," she said cutting him with her eyes.

"Please get your crazy-ass in the car and let's go."

Ten minutes later, they all pulled up one-by-one in front of Joe's house.

"I swear if my mom didn't make those little bacon cups, I'ma flip. That's all I've been thinking about since you said breakfast."

"My fat mama loves bacon."

"I got your fat," Gabrielle said hitting him in the arm.

"I was talking about the baby."

"Yeah, okay," she said getting out of the car. When she looked up toward the house, all she could see was a sea of pink. "This the cutest shit I've ever seen." She covered her face, but she couldn't help but let her tears fall.

"Welcome to your baby shower, babe," K-2 said kissing her on the cheek.

"You knew about this?"

"Who you think put this shit together?" he asked motioning toward all the balloons, streamers, and banners with their daughter's name on it.

"My mama."

"Okay, but who do you think helped?"

"Thank you, baby. This is beautiful."

"Anything for my princesses."

Hearing all of the commotion outside, Joe and Isabella came to welcome their guests.

"You guys didn't have to do all of this," Gabrielle said walking up toward the front door.

"Of course we did," Isabella said hugging her, "Now you go inside and put on the crown and sash I got you."

"Mom, I'm not 12."

"No sash, no gifts."

"Now, where'd you say it was?" she asked walking inside.

"Right there in the living room." Gabrielle was floored by all the effort her mother had went through as she graciously placed the crystal tiara and pink sash on.

"I got the brunch buffet all set up in the kitchen. We have pink velvet waffles, an omelet station, buttermilk biscuits, shrimp and cheese grits, roasted potatoes…"

"Mom, don't you think that's a lot of food for just us? Who else is supposed to be coming?"

"Raquel is on her way now, and I saw Nicole's mom at Whole Foods the other day, so I was able to invite Nicole, Tania, Roxanne, Mya, and Keisha."

Ever since she and K-2 really decided to settle down and move to the Bay, Gabrielle had lost contact with her most of her friends. At 19, they were all worried about where the next function was, but her life was so different now. Providing for her family was all she cared about, but it was going to be nice to be carefree again at least for a little while.

"Oh my god, Mom, thank you so much," she said kissing her on the cheek, "I haven't seen those hoes in forever."

"I got everything covered, so just go and relax. I even have virgin mimosas in there on the tray," Isabella said pointing into the living room.

"What's a virgin mimosa?" Gabrielle asked looking back.

"Orange juice in a fancy glass," she laughed.

"There he is," Joe said as Jewel walked inside holding Chase in his arms, "You can go put him down in the guestroom, son."

"I swear this is all he does," Reagan said walking in with Jailen right beside her.

"He's growing," he said giving her a hug, "Hey, J."

"Hey, Grandpa."

"You hungry?"

"Yes, sir."

"Well, there's plenty of food in the kitchen. Go get you some."

"Are there any pancakes?"

"I got a secret stash just for you," he whispered, "Go ask your grandma Izzy."

"Thanks, Grandpa," Jailen said not needing to be told twice.

"Hey, Joe, you remember my sister Kiko and her husband Sacario, right?" K-2 asked coming in next.

"Yeah, how ya'll doing?"

"Good, sir, and this is my friend Hassan," Sacario said.

"Very nice to meet you, son."

"Ya'll go get something to eat. There's plenty of food in the kitchen."

"Dad, can you hook the game up in the play room?" Gabrielle asked with a small plate full of bacon cups filled with eggs, green onions, and cheese, "I know the kids are gonna get bored."

"Yeah, Keith, why don't you give me a hand?"

"Yes, sir," he said following behind him.

"There's some mimosas in the living room, guys. Help yourself," Isabella said as Jewel and Reagan came out of the guestroom.

"That's the last thing I need." Kiko rubbed her head at the thought of drinking anymore.

"Don't worry, it's just orange juice," Gabrielle said continuing to eat.

"Jewel, can I talk to you?" Reagan asked pulling him to the side.

"Yeah, what's up?"

"Can we go outside please?" He followed her as she walked toward the front door. "Listen," she said closing it behind them, "I know I was beyond gone last night, but I do remember everything that happened before I threw up my pill."

"Reagan, like I said, you were in your feelings. You don't need to keep talking about it."

"See, Jewel that's your problem now. You never want to talk about anything. No matter what happens, you want to pretend like it didn't. I can't do that shit anymore."

"What do you want me to say?"

"I want you to say that you miss Pop. I want you to say that you're not happy. I want you to say what everybody else can see but you."

"What does that do, Rea? Would that bring him back?"

"No, but at least you would be being honest with yourself."

"After Pop died, this street shit seemed frivolous to me. With you just having Chase and with Jailen being there, I thought that I needed to be this certain type of man in order to be a good father. I could never put money over my family. It doesn't mean that much to me, but how can I truly let go of the only thing I know? It runs through my veins. I love my dad, but Golden was the only father figure I had growing up. He taught me what it meant to be a man, how to provide for my family, how to make my money work for me. I broke bread with him and my brothers every single day for years, but I was so quick to turn my back on them. I feel guilty."

"What do you want, Jewel?" Reagan asked already knowing the answer.

"I wanna see my mom. I'm not saying that I want back in, but I want to find out the truth once and for all."

"Jewel, I could never keep you from your family. If this is something you need to do to finally heal yourself then I'm there with you one-hundred percent."

"I know that we were supposed to go on our honeymoon..."

"We'll figure it out, Jewel. This is more important."

"I love you."

"I love you too."

$$$$$

"Didn't you get enough last night?" Paula asked taking the exit that led to Joe's house.

"Mom, what are you talking about?"

"I love that you're spending more time with Jailen, but don't you think that Jewel should be able to have him on his days without you constantly tagging along?"

"I don't see Jewel complaining," Diamond said rolling her eyes.

"But that's just it, Diamond. He is complaining. He's married now. Whatever ya'll had in the past is in the past now. You have to let him go."

"Why does everybody keep telling me that?"

"Maybe because it's true."

"Yes, Jewel is married now, but I am the only woman who he has a kid with. I need him to see that I've changed. My time with Marcus was a dark one, but I'm not in that place anymore. We never got the chance to work on our issues. I just want that chance."

"Diamond, you're not gonna get it by pretending to be friends with that girl. I didn't think that it would go this far, but don't you think that after being the maid of honor at her wedding, reality would have set in?"

"I don't expect you to understand, Mom, but I would do anything to get my family back together, and if Reagan happens to be a casualty in that, oh well."

"I just don't want to see you get hurt again," Paula said pulling up in front of Joe's house.

"Mom, I'm not going to relapse because of Jewel. That's the whole point. I need him to see that I've changed and that Reagan was just a temporary replacement. She was just keeping my seat warm."

"Just be careful, baby," Paula said shaking her head at her daughter's delusions.

"May the best woman win."

"So what time do you need me to come back?" she asked hoping to bring her back to reality.

"I don't. When I took my car into the shop this morning, they said I should be able to pick it up after 6:30 p.m."

"And you don't need a ride?"

"Nope, I'ma ask Jewel to drop me off."

"Is Jailen coming home today?"

"Yeah," Diamond said getting out of the car.

"Okay, I'll see you guys later."

"Bye."

$$$$$

"Are you serious, Reagan? What is she doing here?" Jewel asked noticing Diamond walking up the driveway with a big white gift bag in her hand.

"I invited her last night. Don't be mad, okay? I promise after this, I'ma fall back. Just be nice. Today is about Gabby," she hurried to say.

"If she does one thing, I'ma flip. I'm done with the games, Rea. You better tell her to be on her mothafucking best behavior."

"I will."

"Hey, what ya'll doing out here?" Diamond asked as she climbed the short flight of stairs in her six-inch stilettos.

"We were just hanging up a few last minute balloons and stuff," Reagan lied.

"You need any more help?"

"Naw, we're done now."

"Where's Jailen?" she asked focusing her attention on Jewel.

"In the house with the kids. They're in the play room," he said walking back inside the house, "Ay, I gotta go make a phone call." He disappeared upstairs into Joe's office still mad about Diamond giving Reagan a pill, but he decided to keep his comments to himself for now.

"What's his problem?" she asked sensing the animosity.

"He's still hung over," Reagan said closing the door behind them, "I think you can put your gift in here."

"Okay," Diamond said going to find the pile of presents that already sat against the wall.

"You hungry?"

"No, not right now. Thank you though."

"K, I'ma go make Chase a plate," Reagan said walking into the kitchen.

"Where'd Jewel go?" K-2 asked as soon as she walked in.

"He went to go make a phone call."

"Ay, is Diamond coming through?" Hassan asked taking a bite of his pink velvet waffle with whipped cream on top.

"You like her, huh?" Reagan asked smiling.

"I was just making conversation," he said smiling back showing off his perfectly white teeth. He knew how Sacario felt about the situation, but that didn't stop him from feeling her anyway.

"She's actually here right now. I can go get her for you if you want," she said beginning to walk back into the living room.

"I was just playing," he said pulling her back into the kitchen.

"Don't be scared," she teased.

"Don't be scared of what?" Sacario asked as he entered the kitchen.

He was turnt up the night before, but he made a mental note to talk to Hassan about Diamond. He could tell that he was blinded by her beauty, but he wouldn't feel right if he didn't know the truth about her.

"Nothing," they said in unison.

$$$$$

Twenty minutes later, and Jewel was still tucked off in Joe's office staring down at his phone. He had wanted answers from his mother for years, but now, he felt like he had even more questions than before. He slowly slid his finger across the screen allowing his phone to dial. His heart was beating out of his chest, but there was no turning back.

"Jewel?" Laura asked answering on the first ring.

"Hey."

"I'm so glad you called. I got scared that after our dinner the other night that you wanted nothing to do with me."

"Could you blame me?"

"No, I guess not, but there's a lot you still don't know about, Jewel. I know that it has been a very long time, but everything I did, I did for you."

"You and Pops left me on my own at 15 to fend for myself like a grown-ass man. Tell me how that was for me?"

"But you were never by yourself, Jewel. Golden was there every step of the way."

"Why didn't you tell me? Fuck it, why didn't he tell me? He had more than enough opportunity to look me in the eye and tell me that we were blood. Do you know what that would have done for me back then?"

"It was complicated, Jewel. You went into this life green as could be. You had to build everything from the ground up. Golden wanted you to learn the code of the streets without having a target on your back for being his successor. He had to train you."

"But why…"

"It worked, didn't it? I know that our methods can be argued as unorthodox, but I did what I had to do to ensure that my son could take over this empire someday, and I haven't been as sure as I am today."

"Mom, what do you want from me?"

"I want you to meet me in Barbados tomorrow. Everything has been paid for. All I need you to do is show up."

"I have my own money. I don't need you paying for me."

"Jewel, I've been invisible for the last fifteen years almost. Let me take care of a few things for a change. I know that now, not a lot makes sense, but I promise that after this trip, everything will fall into place. I'll have my driver pick you, Reagan, and the kids up from the airport, okay?"

"I think I'm gonna leave the kids with Joe."

"Oh," Laura said trying not to sound offended, "Maybe next time then."

"Yeah, this is more business for me than anything else. I would just feel better if they're not there."

"I understand, Jewel," she said sighing, "So you and your father are fairly close now, huh?"

"I mean I guess you could say that. We've been through a lot in this past year. It wasn't easy, but I think we're in a better place now than we've ever been before."

"Well, call me when you arrive at the airport," Laura said ignoring the sentiments about his father. She still hated Joe for destroying their family, but her focus was on getting her son back.

"Okay, I'll talk to you later," Jewel said hanging up.

$$$$$

"Thank you guys so much," Gabrielle said unwrapping her next gift, "Awwww, I love it."

"It's a Graco baby swing," her sister Raquel beamed with excitement.

"Thank you, sissy."

"Love you."

"The next one is from us," Isabella said handing Gabrielle a large manila envelope. She quickly pulled out the paper that sat inside.

"It's a picture of a crib," she said confused.

"Not just any crib, but the Angelina crib you saw at Posh Tots. It was way too big to have delivered here, so we had them set it up at your place in the baby's nursery."

"Mom, that crib was like $3,000."

"Nothing is too good for our first granddaughter," Joe said kissing her on top of her head.

"Thank you, everyone, for all the gifts. I have no idea how we're even gonna get all this back to the Bay." She looked around at all of her friends and family whom surrounded her and couldn't help but smile.

"Oh, we'll find a way," K-2 chimed in.

"Keith and I really appreciate all the love," she continued lacing her fingers within his, "We are very excited to welcome our little princess into the world, but we are even more excited to be bringing Naveah into a world surrounded by such loving and supportive people, so thank you again."

"I have to go to the bathroom," Diamond whispered to Reagan, "I'll be right back."

"Okay."

Diamond thought Gabrielle was a sweet girl, but she couldn't help but envy her life. When she looked at her, she saw herself. The only difference was that she didn't get the chance to share the joys of giving birth to her son with her friends and family. She did everything on her own, but there wasn't a day that went by where she didn't wish things were different. As she ascended the stairs to the bathroom lost in thought, she couldn't help but wonder where Jewel was. It seemed like he had disappeared, so she was stuck with Reagan the whole time. Deep down, Diamond didn't have a problem with her. Under different circumstances, she imagined that they could be real friends, but the reality remained that she would always be her competition when it came to Jewel.

After touching up her makeup, she washed her hands and headed out of the bathroom when she ran right into Jewel. "There you are. I've been looking for you all day."

"Well, here I am. What's up?" he asked as he began to walk down the stairs to find Reagan.

"Jewel, can you stop and talk to me for two seconds?"

"What is it, Diamond?"

"I talked to Jailen, and he said that he wants to spend the night over here."

"That works cause me and Reagan actually have something to do tomorrow, so either you or Paula can pick him up from over here. Was that it?"

"No," she said biting the inside of her lip, "Why can't you talk to me without looking like I'm fucking holding you hostage? Damn, everything I do annoys you."

"Look at your track record, D."

"That's the issue, Jewel. You keep holding my past against me. I'm not that person anymore. Whether you recognize it or not, I'm not that person."

"Diamond, by no means do I ever want to take away from your recovery. You had a really rough year last year, and I'm proud that you were able to overcome it. You being a good mother to our son is all I care about, but I still think that you have these delusions that one day we're gonna get back together."

"So you don't love me?"

"Man, here you go with this shit," he sighed.

"Just say that you don't love me, and I'll leave you alone."

"You are the mother of my son. I will always have love for you, but no, I'm not in love with you. I love Reagan."

"Reagan, Reagan, Reagan," she snapped, "That's all you ever talk about."

"She's my wife, D. What do you expect?"

"Why are you so stuck on this dumb bitch? It's only a matter of time before she does something like fuck another one of your friends again."

"If it's all that then why are you even around her?"

"Because I want my family back, and I won't stop until I get it," she said pulling him into her and placing her lips upon his. Caught up in the moment, she melted into their embrace. She wanted him to feel everything she did, but just before he could snatch her off him, Kiko and Gabrielle came walking out of her room.

I knew it, Kiko thought, *You can't trust none of these bitches.*

"Oh, ummmm," Gabrielle said stopping dead in her tracks, "Sorry, I left...uh...something in my room."

"What the fuck?" Jewel asked wiping his mouth off, "It's not what it looks like, Gabby."

"Ok," she said wobbling to the stairs. Not wanting to get in the middle of their drama, they headed down with a stack of diapers filled with melted chocolate bars for another baby game.

"Tell her," Jewel yelled.

"Tell who what?" Diamond asked embarrassed by her actions.

"Reagan," he said pulling her down the stairs by her arm. He knew that Gabrielle wasn't the messy kind when it came to family, but he didn't want to give her the opportunity to tell Reagan what he had been trying to say all along. He deserved that satisfaction.

"Owwww, Jewel, you're hurting me," she said trying to snatch her arm back, but his grip only got tighter.

"Tell her," he yelled again as he threw her in the middle of the living room.

"Jewel, what's going on?" Reagan asked standing up. The fire in his eyes scared her.

"Tell her."

"Can we go outside?" Diamond asked still biting her lip.

"Who wants cake?" Isabella asked trying to distract everyone from the drama.

"I'll help you, Mom." Gabrielle walked with her into the kitchen as Jewel, Reagan, and Diamond went outside.

"What's all this about?" Reagan asked looking at Jewel, but he remained silent.

"For over the past year, me and you have gotten really close on the strength of our kids," Diamond started, "and as much as I appreciate that, I can't deny the fact that I want my family back."

"Wait, what?"

"I'm still in love with Jewel," she finally admitted.

"All this time, I tried to tell you she wasn't really your friend. She's just a conniving bitch."

"Jewel, let me handle this," Reagan snapped, "For the record, Diamond, I'm not as stupid as you like to pretend I am. I know what I got, so believe me, I understand what you lost, but for the sake of my family, I swallowed everything. I never had to worry about Jewel messing around with you behind my back because if he wanted to be with you, he would be. You're so pathetic, but now that everything is out in the open, I guess there's no need to pretend anymore, huh?"

She turned around and walked back inside to join the shower leaving Diamond and Jewel alone. Although she wanted to, she refused to snatch her up. She had already won.

"We obviously can't do this co-parent shit until you realize that what me and you had is done. Yes, we made a beautiful child together, and because of that, we'll be tied to each other for life, but I'm not jeopardizing my marriage for you or anyone else. I've been through hell and back to be with Reagan, and that's where I intend to stay. I want you to be happy, Diamond, I do, but it's really not with me," he said walking inside and closing the door.

She stood in the middle of the driveway with tears rolling down her face. Even more embarrassed by his rejection, she quickly pulled her phone out of her purse and dialed Paula's number. The phone rang and rang, but there was no answer. With her car being in the shop, Diamond had no other choice but to call a cab.

"You good?" Hassan asked walking outside.

"Yeah," she said as she wiped the tears that continued to fall.

"You sure?"

"I'm just waiting for Uber."

"If you need a ride home, mama, I can take you. I was about to get out of here anyway. Sacario's my boy and all, but baby showers aren't really my thing."

"You sure? I don't want to take you out of your way."

"Where you live?"

"In Elk Grove."

"It's good. I can just take the back way home."

"Thank you," she said not knowing what else to say as they walked to his truck.

"Yo, what was all that about?"

"What do you think?"

"Well, whatever it was, it's wasn't a good look, baby," Hassan said pulling out of the driveway as the Jacka flowed through the speakers.

"Listen, I appreciate the ride and all, but please don't assume to know anything about me or my situation."

"Why don't you fill me in then?"

Having no one else to vent to, Diamond began, "Me and Jewel were high school sweethearts. In our senior year, I got pregnant, but because I was so young, my mom sent me to live in Virginia with my grandparents. I graduated high school, had my son, and then a few years later graduated college."

"That's what's up. Where'd you go to school?"

"Norfolk State."

"Oh, okay, I went to Howard. What you study?"

"Nursing," Diamond said sighing a little, "Because I left Sac so suddenly, I never told Jewel that he was going to be a father, so for eight years, he never knew."

"Damn."

"I came back into town a few years ago, and I randomly ran into him one day. I knew I had to tell him that he had a son."

"How'd he take it?"

"He was ecstatic, and even though he was coming out of this thing with Reagan, we decided to start working on us again."

"So you were the side chick and the baby mama?" Hassan asked as he couldn't help but laugh.

"Don't play with me like that," Diamond said in all seriousness, "They had been broken up for like six months before me and him started dating again, and we have a child together, so who really came first? Get your facts straight. Ain't nothing sideline about me."

"My bad, lil mama, I was just joking."

"Play with somebody else," she said folding her arms across her chest.

"So how did you get from that to this?" Hassan asked hoping to save the conversation.

"Jewel is affiliated with the same people you are, and because of that my son and I were kidnapped and almost murdered a couple years ago on the strength of someone wanting to hurt him. It was too much for me to handle at the time, so I told Jewel that I needed break. That was the biggest mistake of my life."

"Why?"

"Cause that left the door open for that bitch to come back. He swore up and down that he was done with her, but the first chance he got to go back, he took it. Losing Jewel felt like I was losing my family all over again, and I didn't want to live through it a second time. After we were really done though, I got mixed up with a really bad guy, and eventually, he made me not care about anything. I was so numb to the world that nothing mattered, not even my own son. I lost myself, and Jewel hated me for it. Well, he still hates me. I just want him to see how much I've changed."

"Why does his approval mean so much to you?" Hassan asked as he entered the freeway.

"Jewel is a standup guy, and I couldn't ask for a better father for my son. After dealing with the last guy I dealt with, I guess I just don't think that there's anybody else out there for me."

"So you just gon' chase behind a nigga who clearly doesn't want you for the rest of your life?"

"I don't expect for you to understand," Diamond said rolling her eyes.

"I don't have any kids, but a lot of my niggas do, so I see all the baby mama drama. That shit ain't gon' get no better. Do you think that if it wouldn't have gone all bad between ya'll that he still wouldn't have gotten back with 'ol girl?"

"Yes, I mean maybe," she said thinking about it. As much as she loved Jewel, she knew that he would never love her as much as he loved Reagan. "It's a pride thing I guess. This bitch has dragged him through the dirt, but no matter what she did, he never stopped loving her. I just feel like I'm such a better woman for him than she is, and I want him to see that."

"From what I see, you're a very beautiful and smart woman who just lost sight of that. There's no reason to compete with anybody. You just gotta get back to what makes you you."

"What if I don't know how to?"

"Maybe I can help you," he said looking her in the eyes.

"Why would you wanna do that?" Diamond laughed nervously.

"There's something about you."

"Take the next exit," Diamond said blushing. She never truly looked at Hassan because all she could see was Jewel, but she had to admit that he was really attractive.

"I know with Jewel being your baby daddy and everything, the situation can get messy, but I'm willing to take that chance. Let me help you take your mind off him," he said forgetting his vow.

"You're saying that like you assume you can."

"Let me try."

"My apartment is up there to the right," she said pointing toward a huge, black iron gate, "You can park right here." Hassan stopped alongside a playground and turned off his ignition. "I'm flattered, I really am, but I don't think you want these problems, baby."

"I'm honestly not worried about Jewel," he admitted.

"No, not that."

"Then what?"

"When I was in my last relationship, I used everything under the sun. Xanax, hop, x, Percocet, coke, molly. You name it, I've tried it. There became a point where my addiction took over my entire life. I lost my self-respect, my job, my family, and it wasn't until I hit rock bottom that I realized I needed to get my shit together."

"Everyone has a past. There's plenty of shit that I've done that I'm not necessarily proud of, but that doesn't define who I am today. I don't care about what you had going on then. I'm interested in getting to know the woman sitting in front of me now," he said grabbing her hand, "Let me take you out on a real date."

"I don't know," she said hesitant about playing too close to home.

"Look, put my number in your phone. When you call me, we'll go from there."

"When, huh? Don't you mean if I call you?"

"I know what I said," he said smiling.

"What is it?" she asked pulling out her cell.

"510-426-8913."

"Well, thank you for the ride," she said getting out of the car as she typed in the last digit.

"I'll be waiting for that call, beautiful."

Sasha Ravae

"Bye, Hassan," Diamond said quickly turning around trying to hide her smile as she floated into the complex.

Chapter 8

"Good morning," Jewel said as he noticed Reagan stirring in her sleep.

"What time is it?" she asked peeking her head from underneath the covers.

"5 a.m."

"The sun isn't even out. Why are you up so early?"

"I didn't get a chance to pack last night after we got home, so I'm doing it now. Our plane leaves in a few hours, Rea."

"I know, Jewel," she said realizing she wasn't going back to sleep any time soon, "I'm up."

"Do you have your stuff ready?"

"Yeah, I just need to call my job."

"For what? I thought you took a few weeks off?"

"I did, but I didn't know that I was leaving today today. I just need to check in."

"All of a sudden, you have to check in? Man," he said shaking his head.

"What?"

"Nothing, I just know how you get."

"Please let me know how I get, Jewel," she said sitting back down on the bed.

"Rea, I know that you think the first chance I get I'ma go back to slanging packs, but that's not the case. I haven't seen my mom in years. I just want to get the answers I feel I deserve."

"Why couldn't we bring the kids then? Why'd they have to stay at your dad's?"

"They didn't have to do anything. Before the shit popped off yesterday, Jailen had already asked Diamond if he could spend the night. He got a few lil homies around there in the neighborhood, and you know Chase is his shadow, so he wasn't leaving. I don't see what the problem is," he said continuing to fold and pack his clothes.

"I just have a bad feeling about this, Jewel."

"Listen, I know my mother isn't the warmest woman in the world, but it's not gonna be that bad."

"Jewel..."

"Do you trust me?"

"What?"

"Do you trust me?"

"With my life," Reagan admitted.

"Okay then, the sole purpose for this trip is to reconnect with my fam hopefully. You gotta think, I've spent half my life around Golden and his family, and never did I know that we were related. Who knows what else this woman has been hiding from me?"

"What part of Barbados are we going to?"

"Some city called Bridgetown," Jewel said picking up their plane tickets from off the dresser.

"Never heard of it."

"Shit, me either, but it's supposed to be near a beach, so I guess that kinda counts as a honeymoon."

"Yeah, with your mom," Reagan said laughing, "I'ma go grab some cereal right quick. You need anything?"

"Naw, I'm good, babe. Thanks, but hurry up though. You still gotta get dressed."

"I know. I know," she said running down the stairs. She couldn't get out of the room fast enough.

As much as she wanted Jewel to deal with all of the issues from his childhood, she was scared where that path would lead him. He was able to let go of the M.A.C. Boys because without Brandon, Golden, or Pop, he didn't feel connected anymore, but with him being Golden's actual nephew, she knew that the life would soon be calling again. When he stepped down as general, she couldn't be happier. She finally felt like she had all of Jewel, and she didn't feel like sharing him again.

Even though she wasn't hungry, she grabbed the milk out of the fridge and the cereal out of the cabinet to keep up appearances before she sat down and watched the clock *tick, tick, tick*.

"You're over thinking this, Reagan. Relax," she said softly to herself.

She couldn't help but think back to how she felt being with Styles when he was in the game. Even at such a young age, she feared for his life every day. She never understood why he put everything on the line all for a dollar. After he went to college, she swore that she would never deal with him being a d-boy ever again, but she had no idea that she would end up marrying one. Jewel's chosen occupation put a strain on their relationship before, and Reagan wasn't ready for history to repeat itself.

"Rea?" he yelled from the top of the stairs.

"Yes, baby?"

"Can you grab my clippers from the downstairs bathroom?"

"Yeah, give me a minute," she said fixing her face. As much as she feared the outcome of their trip, she would never let him know it.

After grabbing Jewel's clipper set from the bathroom cabinet, she headed up the stairs trying to prepare herself for the day. "It'll all work out. I have absolutely nothing to worry about."

$$$$$

Later That Night...

"Took you long enough," Sacario said getting in Hassan's truck.

"My bad, blood, I had some shit to handle."

"More important than this?"

"Naw, never that, so what's the plan?"

"Armani and PJ said they caught up with a few niggas Freddy runs with, but he has been M.I.A. like a mothafucka."

"Typical bitch-nigga shit, bruh. What did you expect? I feel like we're wasting our time."

"I was really ready to go to war just based on the disrespect of them involving K into some shit that he has nothing to do with, but after seeing how these little niggas operate, I can tell they not bout that life."

"So what's the alternative then, chief?"

"I say we just make a formal introduction. Jay hit me up a little while ago and said that he heard Freddy was at La Bamba, so let's go pay him a quick visit."

Ten minutes later, Hassan slowly pulled up across the street from the small Mexican restaurant giving him and Sacario enough time to access the situation.

"You see him?" Sacario asked throwing his black leather jacket over his hoody.

"Hell yeah, that's him in there with the little bitch with purple hair, right?"

"Yeah, that's him."

"You ready?"

"Yep," Sacario said bouncing out.

They waited until a few cars passed before they crossed the darkened street.

Sasha Ravae

"Ay, who is this?" Hassan heard Freddy's friend standing outside ask as they rushed straight to them.

"You know who I am, right?" Sacario asked walking into the restaurant right up to Freddy as he sat down at a table full of tacos. His friend instantly tried to walk back in, but Hassan's pistol met his temple before he could.

"Naw," Freddy said trying to play it cool, "Am I supposed to?"

"Well, let me introduce myself then. "I'm Sacario James. You've probably heard of my clique before. I can guarantee that."

"Who you run with?" he asked playing dumb.

"Money. Always. Coming."

"Never heard of it," he laughed.

"That's funny cause a few days ago, my brother's shop was shot up, and word around town is that you and your bitch-ass potnahs were behind it," Sacario said looking at Freddy's friend D-Rob.

"Like I said, breh, I've never heard of you or the niggas you claim, and I fa sho don't know shit about no shop being shot up, so get the fuck out of my face," he said trying to get up.

"Fred, let's go," his girlfriend said as she saw Sacario reach for his waist.

"Chill, baby, this chinky-eyed mothafucka don't pump no fear in me," he said wanting to reassure her, "What's up, blood? What you bout to do in front of all these people?"

"Not a fucking thing," D-Rob spat, "We don't know about no F.A.G. shit over around these parts. It's the mob on mine, my nigga."

"Wrong answer," Hassan said losing his patience as he held the door open. He knew that because they were younger, Sacario wanted to try and talk some sense into them, but he quickly realized that they weren't about talking. Without saying anything else, he grabbed D-Rob by his dreads and slammed his head into the metal door frame. Taking his lead, Sacario rushed Freddy, pulled out his gun, and whipped it across his face. His girlfriend ran to get help as his blood leaked across the linoleum.

"Nigga, all you had to do was listen," he said continuing to take out his frustrations on his face as tortillas, steak, cheese, and lettuce spilled to the floor. Freddy tried to claw at Sacario hoping to get some sort of relief, but all he could get a hold of was his chain. Sacario looked over and saw Hassan giving it to his potnah who by then was unconscious. His face was swollen and blood ran down his face.

"Like I said, nigga, the M.A.C. Boys aren't going anywhere no time soon. We out here, bruh, so you're only option is to get with it or become a mothafucking spectator, my nigga. Like I said before, the shop you shot up was my brother's place. Only on the strength that that bitch was empty is why I'm letting you walk out of here with your life, but if I ever see you, your potnah, or anybody you fuck with again, I will kill you. That's on my daughter," Sacario said spitting on the ground beside his head before pulling Hassan off of his unworthy opponent, "Come on, blood, these little niggas know not to play with the big boys from now on. Let's go."

When they got back to Hassan's car, they hopped in, and he quickly pulled off into traffic. A crowd formed around Freddy and D-Rob as the fear-filled restaurant owners came out of hiding and called for help. Sacario and Hassan weren't worried about Freddy talking to the police though. They had made their message loud and clear.

As Hassan drove, he pulled out a small container of Purex wipes from the middle console. He wiped off the blood that covered his hands before handing the roll to Sacario.

"I think we're good," he said breaking the silence, "They gon' be too busy picking up their teeth to do anything else."

"So what's up with you and Diamond, blood?" Sacario asked not seeing a better time. The clique shit could wait.

"What you mean?"

"Nigga, don't play dumb. I know you took her home yesterday."

"How you know?"

"Kiko said she saw your car pull off around the same time the drama stopped, so I knew Diamond had to be gone."

"You my boy, so I'm not gon' play like that. I'm digging her. I know that it's a little against protocol..."

"A little? Do you know what she put that nigga Jewel through? They still ain't right."

"I don't know, bruh. I don't see all of that extra shit when I look at her."

"That's the problem now. You shouldn't be even looking at her like that."

"The heart wants what the heart wants," Hassan said laughing.

"Listen to how you sound right now. That pussy must be fire," Sacario said shaking his head.

"I didn't smash."

"What?"

"Nigga, I said I didn't smash. Damn, I just met her."

"So you mean to tell me that you got a little crush or something?"

"Or something," Hassan said not knowing what to make of his feelings either, "I know what you're gonna say already, Cari, but it has nothing to do with Chyna."

"I'm just saying it seems like perfect timing though."

"Me and Chyna weren't even all like that. The bitch wanted a daddy and not the way I'm into, so she had to go. I don't have kids, so my obligation is to myself. I saw Diamond, and she honestly caught my interest, so I'm just weighing out my options at this point. What's the harm in that?"

"She's not an option, my nigga. I can't let you go out like that."

"You can't say she ain't fine though. She look like a young Stacey Dash, no lie."

"It's not about that. They have a kid together. I just don't want you in the middle of their drama. Lil mama got a past."

"Like what?" Hassan asked wanting to see if she had really been honest with him before.

"After some fuck shit happened between Reagan and Jewel, he left, and him and Diamond reconnected. I forgot how it all went down, but this nigga ends up finding out that he had a son after like eight years. They were cool for a minute. Diamond was on her shit. She was a nurse working at Kaiser, so she had her own little dough, feel me? To make a long story short, some shit went down, and Diamond and Jailen were hurt in the process. Jewel loved her, so he went crazy, and he was willing to do whatever it took to make sure that they were straight. Golden called me and K down, and of course we put in work. Luckily, they were okay, but Jewel and her never bounced back from that. Somehow Reagan came back into the picture, and after that, all hell broke loose. Jewel and Diamond broke up, and she lost her mind. She started fucking with this rich white boy, and he turned her out. She was off everything..."

"Sacario, bruh, this sounds like some *Days of Our Lives* type shit. I'm not into all this gossiping, my nigga."

"It's fact, Sani."

"Be that as it may, I'm not bout to chop up this nigga, and how he was or wasn't with Diamond. I just know how I'm trying to be. It would be different if they were still together or even just fucking around, but I mean he is married, right?"

"Yeah, but it's more complicated than that."

"I appreciate you, bruh bruh, I do, but I got this. Trust me, okay?"

"Listen, with everything going on right now, I just don't want this to affect business. At the end of the day, money is the motive, but I don't know how long you can focus on that when you're blinded by Diamond."

"Trust me," he said again, "I got this."

$$$$$

After almost twenty-four hours of traveling, Jewel and Reagan were exhausted once they arrived at Grantly Adams International Airport.

"You good," he asked noticing she still wasn't saying much.

"Yeah, I'm good, just tired."

"You damn near slept the whole way here," he said grabbing their luggage from off of the small metal conveyor belt that went around and around.

"What else was I supposed to do, Jewel?" she asked snatching her bag out of his hand.

"Did I do something?" he finally asked. Her distain for his presence was obvious at this point.

"No, I mean…it's just…"

"It's just what?" he asked pulling her off to the side.

"I'm…"

"Jewel," they both heard someone yell behind them.

"Hey," he could barely say before Laura wrapped her arms tightly around him.

"You have no idea how long I've been wanting to do this."

"How are you?" he asked smiling a little.

"Better now that you're here."

"You remember Reagan, don't you?"

"Of course, how could I forget a face as pretty as hers?"

"Nice to see you again, Ms. Smith."

"Call me Mom," she winked, "I've always wanted a daughter."

"You drove here?" Jewel asked ready to get out of the crowded airport. All he wanted to do was lay down.

"Of course not," she said in shock, "Do I look like I drive?"

"Sorry, I forgot who I was talking to."

"My driver Kurt is waiting outside of the airport. He was supposed to come in and get you, but I couldn't wait," Laura said as she led them to the car.

Tourists of all shades and colors hurried past them as Jewel tried to make sense of it all. He remembered going to Barbados as a kid but not much else.

"Welcome to Bridgetown," Kurt said taking off his small black hat as he helped Jewel and Reagan with their bags.

"Jewel, this is my driver Kurt. Kurt, this is my not so little boy Jewel."

"Nice to meet you, man."

"Nice to see you again, I should say. I remember when you were this high," he said pointing down at his knee in a Bajan accent.

"I'm sorry I don't remember you," Jewel said trying to think back, but everything was a blur. He had spent half his life trying to pretend as if his mother and father never existed, so it was going to be hard to embrace everything all at once.

"That's quite understandable, Jewel. You have been gone from the family throne for a long time now. It's just nice to have you home."

"Home?"

"Let's go, Kurt. We have a busy day ahead," Laura said interrupting.

"Man, I know we have a lot to get to, but me and Reagan are beat. You think we can hook up later?"

"Hook up? Jewel speak like you have some type of sense about yourself, my goodness, and no, we cannot postpone this. I have family coming, so it's very important that you be present," she said as Kurt opened her door letting her inside the town car. Knowing it would be a waste of time to argue, Jewel grabbed Reagan's hand and followed suit.

An hour later, they drove up a hill that wrapped around until they reached the top.

"We're here," Laura said with excitement.

"This is where we're staying?" Reagan asked a little taken back as she stared down at the miles of beach beneath them.

"Mom, where are we? Please don't tell me that you did all this because I was coming?" Jewel asked looking around the luscious green covered estate as salt water filled the air.

"Jewel, you can't be serious, dear," she said heartbroken that he had disconnected himself from her so much that he couldn't remember where they came from.

"This is Papa's villa."

"Oh, yeah, okay," he said remembering his grandfather.

"Who's Papa?"

"Papa was my father. A simple fisherman here in Bridgetown, but he worked very hard to provide his family with all of this," she said simply as she motioned toward the fifteen acre estate, "Let's not just sit out here. I had Ana fix us some breakfast."

"Jewel, you did not tell me that we would be staying at your family's resort," Reagan whispered.

"I honestly forgot about this place," he admitted.

"How? If I lived here as a child, I would never wanna leave," she said touching the bright tropical plants that surrounded them.

"If it was just you here, you would."

"What are you two whispering about?" Laura asked looking back as she continued to lead them inside the compound.

"This place is amazing," Reagan said speaking up, "If you don't mind me asking, how much did it cost?"

"I can't say how much Papa paid for it initially, but with all of the upkeep and new additions my brothers Stevin, Golden, and I have made, I would say this place is worth roughly around $32 million."

"Dollars?" Reagan asked in disbelief.

"Yes, dollars, sweetie," Laura said laughing, "It's just money, you know? None of us can take it with us when we go."

"Let me get that for you, Miss Laurie," Kurt said as he hurried to open the front door.

"Thank you, Kurt," she said walking inside.

"Jewel, is that you? I can't believe the time has finally come," a short light-skinned woman dressed in a lime green cover up and sun hat said as she wrapped her arms around his waist.

"Ms. Naidene?"

"Well, I guess it's okay for you to finally call me Aunt Naidene, huh?" she said getting a little teary eyed.

"Why didn't you ever say anything?"

"I couldn't, Jewel. You have to believe that. Golden swore me to secrecy. He always said that if it came out that you were his nephew, there would be a price on your head. He convinced me that you were safer in the dark. You became so close to us over the years that I would've done anything to keep you and my children safe," she said as tears slowly continued to roll down her face, "I know it didn't seem like it, but Golden wanted the best for you too."

"How you holding up?" he asked placing his hand on her shoulder.

"As well as someone who lost their husband can be. I just try and take it one day at a time," she said wiping her eyes, "Anyway, enough about me. Reagan, how are you, sweetheart?"

"I'm good, Ms. Naidene. I feel like I barely got to see you at the wedding," she said giving her a hug.

"Yeah, I heard Laura showed up unannounced, and I wasn't in the mood for the drama," she said rolling her eyes, "After you two said your I do's, I was out of there."

"Naidene, would you stop bothering my son and my new daughter-in-law please?" Laura asked walking back into the foyer.

"How long you guys staying?"

"We haven't decided yet," Jewel said looking at Reagan. He knew how she felt about being there, but already he felt like he could breathe again.

"Well, I hope that this doesn't become just a turnaround trip. We have so much to catch up on."

"And we will," he assured her, "What room are we in? I wanna go put our bags away."

"Pick any one on the second floor. No one was here this past week, so feel free. You two go get washed up and meet us in the dining hall in fifteen?"

"Sounds good, Mom," Jewel said grabbing Reagan's hand as he led her up the stairs.

"Jewel, your mom lives here by herself?" she asked admiring the architecture.

"I don't think so. She has a place in New York. I can't see her living here full time, but you never know," he said picking the first open room he saw, "You need to change or anything?"

"Naw, I'm good. I just have to go to the bathroom," she said walking into the full-size, private room.

"We'll go downstairs and have breakfast and then we can go to the beach or something if you want."

"That's okay, Jewel," Reagan said through the door, "This is about you and your family. I'll occupy myself."

"Naw, baby, this is as much about you as it is about that. We're supposed to be on our honeymoon right now."

"And we will be, but you need to deal with this first, Jewel. I'm okay. I promise."

Ten minutes later, Reagan was still in the bathroom.

"Babe, you good?" Jewel asked as he laid across the bed waiting.

"Yeah, I'm fine. Just go downstairs. I think I'ma take a shower after all. I want to get rid of this airport smell."

"Alright, ask somebody where the dining hall is when you get downstairs. This place is like a maze."

"K, see you in a minute."

Reagan waited for Jewel to leave the room before she walked out as she stared down at the word *Positive* that stretched across the pregnancy test she held in her hand. She knew that Jewel would be ecstatic that they were finally having a child together, but she didn't know if there in Bridgetown was the right place to announce the news.

"I'll tell him when we get home," she smiled to herself as she rubbed her belly. She knew it was early, but she was excited about the life that was growing inside of her.

She walked over to her suitcase and grabbed a pair of loose fitting harem pants, a black tee, black leather pumps, and an olive green kimono. The tropical weather was nice, but she felt bloated, and she needed to keep her secret until they got back home.

"Here goes nothing," she said walking downstairs.

$$$$$

For the rest of the day, Reagan and Jewel joined Laura and Naidene as they explored the estate. Between the game and theater room, the three swimming pools overlooking the beach, the gardens, and Jacuzzis surrounded by Cassia trees, Reagan was beginning to think that she could get used to Barbados after all. Later that night, Laura had her personal chef Ana prepare a feast in honor of Jewel's arrival, and one-by-one estranged family members began to show up ready for all the island festivities. Naidene decided to come early to enjoy a few extra days of R&R, but she was so happy when her children showed up along with her nephew Smackz.

"Jewel," she yelled from the front door. She hoped he was close enough to hear her. Luckily her voice echoed throughout the marble covered mansion.

"Yes, Naidene?" he said coming from out of the kitchen. He had been eating all day, but he couldn't help but sample everything Ana put together. Reagan didn't cook.

"I have a few people I want to formally introduce you to." He immediately started smiling as he approached the front door. "I know that you have known them almost half your life, but let me re-introduce you to your cousins Reyna, Mario, Sergio, Monica, Isaiah, and your uncle Stevin's son Stevin Jr."

"It's Smackz, Auntie Naidene," he said giving Jewel a hug.

"Never will there be a day where I call you Smackz. Go somewhere before I tell your mama," she said popping him in the back of his head, "Where's Sonya anyway?"

"Outside with Pops. We all got out here at the same time."

"I'll be right back," she said grabbing the bottom of her ankle length sundress as she carefully walked outside.

"I don't even know what to say," Reyna said looking down at the ground as she swept her shoulder length curly hair behind her ear, "You have to believe that none of us knew anything about this, Jewel."

"Reyna, I'm not mad at ya'll. Coming here, I can't lie, I was hot. I mean my mom has been ghost for a really long time, and then she just shows up at my wedding."

"Is Reagan here?" Monica asked.

"Yeah, she's upstairs. She had a headache earlier. I think she's laying down now."

"Let me go say hi," she said heading toward the staircase.

"We're in the first room on the second floor."

"K, I'll be right back."

"Anyway, after being here, I just feel at home, you know?"

"Well, that's cause you are, bruh," Mario said giving Jewel a hug next.

"Even though Daddy never mentioned anything really about your mom or the fact that we're all blood that never stopped us from knowing how much he loved you, Jewel," Reyna said getting teary eyed. She really missed Golden.

"I still don't know the full story, but right now I guess I appreciate that I finally get to enjoy my family again."

"We love you, cuz," Smackz laughed.

"Well, hello there niece and nephews," Laura said joining the reunion.

"Hey, Auntie Laura," he said kissing her on the cheek.

"Hi, Laura," Reyna said greeting her estranged aunt.

Due to their father's operations, Laura, Golden, and Stevin grew apart. Golden was the youngest and hated that he lived in his father's shadows. He wanted to make a name for himself, so he moved out to California and set up shop. He was determined to be his own man while Laura and Stevin gladly worked to keep the family business going strong, but they had done so much dirt that they didn't know who they could really trust outside of their circle. Due to their paranoia, Jewel and the rest of his cousins were separated in the process to protect them. None of Golden's children had interest in the game despite their father's notoriety, so when Jewel came along, he was the protégé he had always wanted. But being that Laura and Joe were his parents, his identity as a Smith had to be kept secret until now.

"Where is everybody?"

"Mama, Uncle Stevin, and Auntie Sonya are outside."

"Well, Ana's done with dinner, so you all go put your bags away and meet us in the banquet room."

Without protest, Golden's five children and Smackz walked up to the second floor to pick out their rooms.

"You okay?" Laura asked Jewel as she noticed the confused look on his face.

"Yeah, it's just crazy how I've seen all of G's kids damn near grow up. I've always felt so close to them, but I never imagined that we were related."

"Jewel, after tonight, I promise all of your questions will be answered, okay?"

"I hope so."

"Laurie," they both heard a voice boom into the house.

"Hello, Stevin," she said kissing her younger brother on both cheeks, "How was your flight?"

"Long, but we made it."

"Where you coming from?" Jewel asked.

"Miami."

"Okay, my wife and I flew out from California, so it took us almost a day to get out here. We actually had a layover in Miami."

"Well, now you know that if you're ever in Florida to call your uncle Stevie."

"Most definitely," Jewel said extending his hand, "Nice to meet you."

"Boy, if you don't get over here," he said pulling Jewel into him, "It's so good to finally meet you. Better late than never I guess. Golden always spoke so highly of you."

Jewel looked up at his newfound uncle and couldn't help but notice how similar he and Golden looked. There was no denying that they were brothers.

"This is my wife Sonya."

"Nice to meet you," he said shaking her hand as she walked inside with Naidene.

"Where are the kids?"

"Nicole and Cameron both had to work. You know Cameron just started his residency at Mount Sinai, and Jasmine is finishing up with finals at University of Florida, so I told them I would give their regards. Stevin was the only one who could come of course."

"Yeah, he's up there with the others getting ready for dinner."

"Is it that time already?" Stevin asked looking down at his watch.

"Yes, so ya'll go and freshen up and meet us down in the banquet hall."

"I should probably go and grab Reagan," Jewel said noticing the time too.

"Where is she?"

"Upstairs. She had a headache earlier, so she went to go lay down."

"There should be some aspirins in the cabinet in the bathroom. Give her two. That should help."

"Thanks, Mom," Jewel said running up the stairs.

When he got to their room, the door was slightly cracked, and he could hear Reagan on the phone.

"Thanks so much for keeping the kids, Joe...oh, Diamond came and got Jailen? Well, we should only be out here for a few more days...kiss my baby for me. Okay, talk to you later...bye."

Jewel waited until she hung up before he walked in. "Who was that?"

"Your dad. I called to check on the boys. I guess Diamond went and got Jailen."

Counterfeit *Dreams* 4

"Yeah, I know. Paula texted me earlier. You good?" Jewel asked sitting down next to her.

"I guess I'ma little homesick."

"Homesick? Rea, we just got here."

"Jewel, this is the first time I have been away from my son for more than a few hours."

"Chase is fine. I think you just don't want to be here."

"I'm trying."

"Try harder," he snapped, "My entire world was turned upside down only a few days ago. I know this is an adjustment for you right now, but it's not like I'm asking you to move across the world. I'm just asking for you to be here for me."

Not in the mood to argue, Reagan decided to drop it. Maybe she was putting the cart before the horse. She didn't know what Laura's intentions were when it came to Jewel, but she had to admit so far she had been nothing but perfect.

"What do you need me to do?"

"Just be regular. My mom's brother Stevin and his wife and son are here, and so are Naidene's kids."

"Yeah, Monica came up here a few minutes ago."

"We're just gonna have dinner, and I hope we can finally get to the real reason why my mom asked me here. She's been walking on eggshells."

"That's her walking on eggshells?" Reagan asked fixing her makeup in the mirror.

"Surprisingly, yes," he said laughing.

"I'm sorry, baby, and you're right. I haven't really put a lot of effort into this. I'm just cautious I guess because I want to protect you."

"I'm a big boy, Rea. I can protect myself. I just need you by my side."

"I'm right here, Jewel," she said sitting down on his lap.

"Thank you."

"Ay, J, your mom is looking for you," Smackz said knocking on the door.

"Good looking, bruh," he said scooting Reagan off of him, "Here we come."

95

A few minutes later, they walked downstairs and into the banquet hall. Reagan had met a majority of everyone there already, but never under these circumstances.

Clink. Clink. Clink.

Laura tapped her butter knife softly against her champagne glass as everyone found their seats.

"Before we begin tonight, I would like to give Ana the opportunity to present tonight's meal. It is spectacular as usual."

"Good evening," the small dark-skinned woman, with her head wrapped in a colorful scarf protecting the small twists underneath, said as she approached the table, "Tonight I have prepared for you cutters, conkies, rice 'n peas, sea eggs, souse, crane chubb, grilled pigtails, conch fritters, plantains, and for dessert bread fruit. We also have rum punch, Cockspur's Five Star cocktails, and mauby, which is non-alcoholic. Tonight's courses will be served family-style in honor of the occasion, so enjoy."

"All I heard was plantains," Reagan whispered.

"I don't know what none of that shit is either, but Ana's been feeding me all day, so I know it's gon' be on point," he said rubbing his hands together.

As the servers brought out each course, Laura thought it was time to get down to business.

"Thank you, everyone, for coming out on such short notice. I know that you all may have many questions, and I feel tonight, Stevin and I are obligated to answer them. When Goldie was murdered, our world was completely turned upside down. As my baby brother, we hadn't always been that close, but I loved him nonetheless, and I am so grateful that he watched over my only son for all those years," she said looking at Jewel, "but now that he's gone, there's a hole in our family again."

Naidene picked up her napkin and wiped the tears that began to fall. There wasn't a minute that went by where she didn't think of her husband.

"Maybe I should start from the beginning, so, Jewel, you can hopefully understand where we are now better. My father, your grandfather Nathaniel Smith was born in this country. He grew up very poor here in Bridgetown. His family was full of fisherman, and that's what he expected to be doing for the rest of his life. When he was 17, he worked at his family's port, and this is when he met your other grandfather Joseph Sanchez, Sr. He used to come from the Dominican

Republic on boats and smuggled cocaine through the channels, and eventually, Papa and he became business partners. Their relationship was obviously mutually beneficial. Because Papa had control over the port, Joseph Sr. was able to send pounds and pounds of cocaine to Puerto Rico..."

"Why Puerto Rico?" Jewel asked.

"Shipments from Puerto Rico to the US are not considered international shipments, so they're not given as much attention as others. Because of this lucrative friendship, Papa and Joseph Sr. became close, and in turn, I was promised to your father at a very young age. Papa felt that it was a way to solidify the Smith-Sanchez cartel. At first, Joe and I were hesitant about marrying each other because we had practically grown up together, but for the benefit of both our families, we agreed. When we got married, he was in school for law in California, and I was at NYU for my business degree, but when we graduated, we decided to get a house in El Dorado Hills. Although it seemed like we were legit, Joe's predestined occupation as an Attorney allowed our family's operations to continue flawlessly. He was on our side, but after Isabella got in his head, Joseph Sr. had a conversation with me and told me that in order for the business to survive, I had to let Joe go. He was weak, and even though, he probably never planned on it, his allegiance was then elsewhere. I can't lie and say that Joe deciding to leave defense law alone to go live happily-ever-after with Isabella didn't have a negative effect on me. I was devastated. He and I had been groomed for each other. He was the only other person who knew what our lives really consisted of, and he abandoned me without ever looking back. After our divorce, I was confident that he wouldn't be able to instill in you the values you needed. You were so restless, Jewel. You were looking for some sort of direction, and when you decided to leave home, I knew that Golden was the only person who could teach you about our history. I'll admit, he was more on the grassroots level, but I digress..."

"So when Golden approached me, he already knew who I was?" Jewel asked.

"Of course."

"Why didn't he just tell me we were related then?"

"How could he, Jewel? Despite this new image you've managed to create for yourself over the years, you were born with several silver spoons in your mouth. Pardon the cliché. You had to be stripped of everything in order to build yourself back up, and that's exactly what you did, son. I know that many accused Goldie of favoritism, but if they knew you were the heir to the Smith-Sanchez throne, you would've had way more to worry about then Brandon Edwards and Kisino Brown."

"You knew about that?"

"We can talk about the specifics later, Jewel. I don't think that the dinner table is the most appropriate place, but yes, we know."

"So what's the point of all this?"

"Jewel, you are the connection between the Smith-Sanchez cartel, and it's time you finally take your seat at the head of the table. You grandfather Joseph Sr. has requested to see you."

"About what?" he asked confused. Just like Laura kept her family private, Joe didn't really mention his either.

"Rum punch?" a waiter asked Reagan as she sat and looked at Jewel. She knew what was coming next.

"No, thank you. Can I have a glass of water please?"

"Jewel, baby, that's business. We have time to talk about that later. Tonight we celebrate our family being united as one. Do not ever think that a day went by where you were not missed, but everything happens for a reason. The streets have tested you, and although, you may feel like you've failed, you're exactly where you need to be. This was destined, my love," she said raising her glass, "To my one and only Jewel Noah Sanchez."

"To Jewel," the room repeated.

He didn't know what to make of his mother's revelation. Everything he had, he fought for, but now he knew that it was what she had planned all along.

"J, I think I ate too much," Reagan whispered in his ear, "My stomach hurts. I'ma go lay down."

"I'll go with you."

"No, that's okay. It looks like you have a lot to deal with right now. I'll be okay," she said kissing him on the cheek, "I'll see you in a little bit."

"So that means distribution is still running?" Smackz asked over the low roar of the room, "M.A.C. is set then."

"Stevin, we will talk about the specifics later. Tonight we will just enjoy the fact we are all here together as a family," his father said, "I know Golden and Papa would be proud that the missing piece to the Smith name had been restored."

The servers went around the room passing out strong rum cocktails as Soca music played in the background. Jewel didn't know where his mother's news left him. After seeing Golden and Pop get their lives snatched away from them, he valued the promise he made. He had lost so much that none of it seemed worth it anymore. He gave his word to Reagan that she and their family were his first priority, and he intended on keeping his word. Although, he was flattered by his mother's proposition, he couldn't imagine going back to the life that he tried so hard to run away from.

As the night went on, and the drinks continued to flow, the Smiths used the time to catch up on all that they lost. Jewel had been around Golden's family for years, so being there felt natural to him. He didn't know anything other than them. He was finally at peace.

"You enjoying yourself, baby?" Laura asked walking up to Jewel as he sat out on the balcony.

"Surprisingly, I am. I was nervous coming up here though."

"Why?"

"Because we've never had that mother-son relationship, so I didn't expect this to be any different."

"I know that back then I was hard on you..."

"Hard? You and Pop were nonexistent."

"Your father and I were in a really bad place during that time. He was all I had ever known. I lost my virginity to that man for God's sake. I married him and bore the most beautiful boy anyone could have ever imagined. We sat on top of both of our family's fortunes, and still it wasn't enough. I lost myself, Jewel. I know that many believe I was only with him for the money, but I loved your father. I had my own money. It was never about that, but I'm sorry you got caught in the crossfire. I never intended for that to happen."

"As hard as it is for me to even understand and process all of this, I have to forgive you. Not for you, but for me. I hated Joe for a very long time, and that hate consumed me. It affected a lot in my life, but my worst fear was that it would affect my ability as a father. I don't want to hate your forever."

"I would die if you did, Jewel."

"Still dramatic I see," he said smiling.

"As always," Laura said kissing him on the forehead, "Now, where is this wife of yours? I feel like every time I turn around, she's gone."

Sasha Ravae

"She hasn't been feeling well today. She said her stomach was bothering her at dinner, so she went back to the room."

"Awww, poor baby. Domestic people usually don't do well with long flights. I can go check on her if you want."

"Could you, Mom? I needed to holla at Smackz and Stevin, but I wanted to make sure she was okay first."

"You need to speak with Stevin Jr. and your Uncle Stevin. Jewel, seriously, we are going to have to break this street vernacular you have. Now, go. She'll be fine. I'll head up there right now," Laura said getting up.

"I missed you." He bent down to give her a hug. Her touch sent chills throughout his body as he melted into her embrace. For a moment, he felt at ease in her arms; he wanted the feeling to last forever.

"Go, before you my make me cry all my makeup off, boy," she said wiping the corner of her eyes, "I will see you tomorrow at breakfast." Laura could only imagine the picture Joe had painted of her to Jewel, but she was glad that he was finally opening up again. She feared that she had lost her son forever.

Once Jewel walked off to find Smackz, she walked back into the house and headed toward the second floor to Jewel and Reagan's suite.

Knock. Knock. Knock.

"Jewel?" Reagan asked lifting her head up in the darkened room.

"No, sweetie, it's Laura. Can I come in?"

"Yes, of course," she said turning on the light.

"Jewel said that you hadn't been feeling well today."

"Yeah, I had a headache earlier, and I think I ate too much at dinner or something because I got the worst cramping, but I'm feeling better now."

"How far along are you?"

"Excuse me?" The words didn't even register yet.

"You're pregnant, aren't you? Oh, please excuse my assumptions if I've spoken out of turn," Laura said straightening out her dress as she crossed her legs.

"How did you know?"

"Well, when we had dinner in Sacramento, I believe that you and Jewel were both drinking that night, but today you have been opting for water, and your clothes seem to be a little more loose fitting. How far along are you?"

"Just a few weeks I think."

100

"See, I'm very perceptive, Reagan. There's not a lot that can get past me these days. Have you told Jewel?"

"Not yet. I know that being here is very important to him, and I'm not trying to compete for attention. I'm going to wait until we get back home."

"Well, I am very excited," she said getting up to give her a hug, "Now I will have three grandchildren to spoil."

"Thank you, Laura. You have no idea what it means to have someone to talk to. Jewel has been wrapped up in a lot lately."

"Well, that's what I'm here for, Reagan. I know that I have missed a lot of important moments in his life, but I'm here now. Remember that."

Chapter 9

Two Weeks Later...

"You miss me?"

"Boy, I don't even know your last name," Diamond laughed into the phone.

"Why you just can't go with the flow?" Hassan asked walking to his refrigerator to grab a bottled water, "And it's Williams."

"Look, Mr. Williams, you're nice and all, but you out of all people should know that I don't need to be getting myself into anything too serious. I'm just trying to have fun, you know?"

"I'm not asking you to marry me, Diamond."

"Shit, you acting like it."

"Yeah, okay," Hassan laughed, "People think I need to stay away from you anyway."

"Who's people?"

"Does it matter?"

"No, cause niggas stay yapping about me," Diamond said rolling her eyes, "It had to be Sacario though or that annoying-ass nigga Keith."

"Could've been," he said not about to implicate his potnahs.

"I get it though. They really look out for Jewel, you know? They're just trying to protect him I guess."

"They're trying to protect me," Hassan said lighting a blunt as he laid back on his king-size bed.

"Do you need protecting, Hassan?"

"You tell me," he said in all seriousness.

"Enough about Jewel and me. Why don't you tell me something about you?" she said wanting to change the subject.

"Something like what?"

"Well, for starters, are you single?"

"Would I be on the phone with you right now if I wasn't?"

"So again, are you single? It's 2015, baby."

"Yes, Diamond, I have no baby mamas, girlfriends, jump-offs, freaks, or hoes to speak of."

"Why not?"

"I was dealing with this chick for a minute, but mentally, we weren't on the same page, you know? I know I hustle or whatever, but it's a means to an end. It seems like females hear about my reputation before even meeting me though. I guess I just appreciated that you've never heard about me. It's like I have a clean slate with you."

"I feel the same." For the first time in a long time, she wasn't being condemned for the sins of her past.

"I'm glad I don't have to live up to any unrealistic expectations."

"The hell you don't," Diamond joked.

"You know what I mean."

"Like you said, everybody has a past."

"Now that you're up to speed though, how about we start focusing on our future?"

"And what does that look like?"

"Let me take you out, so you can find out?"

"What you doing Saturday?" she asked not giving herself the chance to say no.

$$\$\$\$\$\$$$

"Jewel, can you meet me in the study in five?" Laura asked walking out to the pool.

"Yeah, what's up?" he asked slipping out of the water.

"Your uncle Stevin and I would like to speak with you about a few things. Hurry now," she said walking back inside.

"I guess I'll go call Chase," Reagan said standing up and wrapping herself with a melon-colored towel. The chlorine water dripped from her hair down to the turquoise-colored glass tile beneath her.

"That's the third time today."

"What else do I have to do?"

"I know what your mouth says, but I'm starting to think you don't really wanna be here. I miss the kids too, but damn, you did plan on going on vacation without Chase being on your tittie, right?"

"This is different."

"Why? Because it's about me?"

"Jewel, I'm not tryna argue with you. Please just go and see what your mom wants."

"Naw, she can wait. I'm dealing with this now."

"There's nothing to deal with. We've been here two weeks already, so now we can go home and everything can go back to normal."

"Reagan, I haven't decided when I'm going back, but I'm enjoying being out the way."

"So what? I'm supposed to leave my son with your dad forever?"

"Don't start."

"No, seriously, Jewel, what's your timeline looking like?"

"I don't have one. Chase and Jailen are fine. Those boys don't want for nothing, and now is no different."

"That's not enough for me, Jewel. I have a responsibility at home. I have a company I'm tryna run. I appreciate the time we spent out here, but I'm not trying to make this my home."

"So you're leaving?"

"Are you coming with me?"

"No," he said walking into the house. For the past fourteen days, the pressures of the world had been lifted from his shoulders. He never felt like he was a part of a family outside of the M.A.C. Boys, but he was happy just being around his own. His mother hadn't been the best in the past, and although Jewel was ready to move forward, he was convinced that Reagan was against it.

He walked up the spiral staircase all the way to the third floor. He remembered that level was off limits when he was a child, but it wasn't hard to find Laura's secret office.

Knock. Knock. Knock.

"Come in, Jewel," he heard her say. He slowly opened the door to see Smackz and Stevin already sitting there. "Have a seat, baby," she said getting up to greet him at the door, "You want anything to drink?"

"Naw, I'm good," he said giving dap to Smackz before he sat down beside him, "What's all this about?"

"I know that these past two weeks have been ideal. I really have enjoyed myself, and I'm very happy that our family has been reunited. All of our deepest, darkest secrets have been exposed, and now, we can finally move past them and ascend into our destiny."

"Okay," Jewel said not understanding her coded language, "So what does that mean?"

"That means that now that we've gotten our bonding time out of the way, we can get down to the real reason why we're all gathered here."

"And that is?" He knew there had to be a catch.

"Jewel, as you know, your uncle Golden was a very influential man. He was able to transform that city and bring many jobs to the people. Some legit and some not, so you can imagine what a lost he was to the community."

"Yeah, niggas took it hard," he said remembering how his lifeless body looked on the cold pavement of his driveway.

"When Golden first announced you as general, his theory was that you would either sink or swim, but as you know, your uncle wasn't ready to take the training wheels off. When he found out that Kisino Brown discovered who you really were, he promised to do anything to protect you even if that meant losing his life." Jewel didn't know what to say. "It was unfortunate what happened to him and your friend Pop."

"He was more than a friend. That was my brother."

"Nonetheless. I appreciated you passing the torch to your associate Sacario James, but I'm thinking we need a complete reorg."

"A re- what?"

"Reorganization. We start from the top to the bottom starting with you," she smiled.

"Why me? I'm not at the top. I'm not even affiliated anymore."

"I hate to break it to you, my love, but you don't get a choice in this. You have both Smith and Sanchez blood running through your veins. This is your calling. Why do you think you been so depressed lately? You have been denying the truest parts of yourself, but I won't allow it any longer. Everything you have endured in the past has enabled you to enter into the promise land today."

"Jewel, what your mother is trying to say is that she's ready for you to take her place at the head of the table."

"I'm not getting any younger, my love. I have built this system from the ground up. All I need is someone to run it for me and that someone is you."

"I don't understand," Jewel said trying to process her request.

"Now that Golden is gone, we need someone there on the streets, and I know that you have faith in this Sacario boy, but Stevin and I have decided that your cousin Stevin Jr. will now head the M.A.C. Boys. He has been a part of your uncle's operations in Sacramento since he was a child. He singlehandedly runs the now three distribution facilities in the area. From a business standpoint, it just makes sense."

"So where does that leave Sacario and the rest of the guys who have laid their lives on the line for Golden each and every day?"

"No, sweetie, you must have misunderstood me. We're looking to reallocate our resources not eliminate. I'm pretty sure we'll find something for Sacario and whoever else."

"And where does this redistribution process leave me?"

"You, my son, will be doing what your uncle and I do now. You are now distribution. No more small time deals, Jewel. Everything goes through you. We're talking about thousands of pounds at a time on average."

"We've seemed to acquire many wealthy business associates over the years, so the infrastructure is already in place," Stevin said.

"Why me?"

"Why not you? Even though you seemed to enjoy your taste of the streets, your father and Golden made sure to keep you financially savvy. You don't own several multi-million dollar properties at your age for no reason. Golden made sure to keep you in the boardroom as much as he kept you on the block as you would say. A majority of my job consists of developing and maintaining client relationships, and if you're anything like your mother, you will have no problem with that. I would like to enjoy finally being a mother again and spending time with my grandchildren, but I need to know that what Papa worked so hard to build will survive. I am confident that with a little guidance, Jewel, we can thrive, but I need you to believe in you like I do."

"I appreciate this, Mom, I do. I never could've imagined that Golden's connect was his own family, and the fact that you're asking me now to take over this role is something that I could have only hoped for…in the past. Being in this life, I have been exposed to a lot, and I've done my fair share of dirt too, but because of my choices, my family has been hurt more than once. I made a promise to Reagan, and to myself, after Pop died that I was done. I'm not hurting for cash now, so choosing that over my family's wellbeing is something I can't do. Reagan is really adamant about me cleaning my life up. I love her too much to even betray her like that again."

"What if I talk to her?"

"What?"

"If all you're looking for is her approval then let me talk to her. This is your birthright, Jewel. There's no way I'm going to let you give that up."

"And what if you can convince her? Then what? I'm supposed to just pack up my family and move to Barbados?"

"You don't have to do that if that's not what you want. This is only one of our family's homes. You can go anywhere you want in the world, my love. Don't think so small. You can even stay in California although I wouldn't recommend it," she said a little biased to the East coast.

"You don't get it, Mom. Golden bred me into a brotherhood. There wasn't anything that I wouldn't have done for any one of my brothers. Shit, even the ones who crossed me," he said thinking about Brandon, "But then one day, he just threw me up on this pedestal, and soon niggas began to look up at me like I was looking down on them, but that was never the case. It was just my view. I had to make decisions to protect people's lives, and all of that pressure eventually became too much to handle. I never wanted to be the nigga giving orders. I just wanted to play my part to ensure that the team kept growing and we kept expanding, but it seems like you tryna throw me right back in the same position Golden did. It's lonely at the top though, Mom."

"So what do you need to feel more comfortable, Jewel?"

"I want my potnahs to come with me."

"Excuse me?"

"My boys Sacario and K-2 have been there for me through a lot. Unfortunately, many of my other folks didn't make it. I can't see myself accepting the title as distro on my own. There needs to be some sort of checks and balance system in place like you and Steve had, so it's either all of us or none at all."

"Jewel, you have to understand it is normally against protocol to bring in outsiders…"

"Well, obviously this isn't a normal situation. If I had been brought up for this exact purpose then you have to trust me."

"He's right, Laurie," Stevin said sitting on the edge of his chair.

"Fine, Jewel, we will discuss that when we go to meet with your grandfather."

"Not so fast, Mom. You still have a little work to do before this meeting. If Reagan says no then that's a deal breaker for me. Get her to say yes, and you got your man."

"Piece of cake," Laura said taking a sip of her ice-cold scotch, "Piece of cake."

$$\$\$\$\$\$$

Later that night, Jewel was still in business mode with Smackz and his uncle Stevin. Reagan had been giving him the silent treatment the whole day, so it was easy to fall back into the familiar, but Laura was on a mission, so she used their distance as a distraction.

Knock. Knock. Knock.

"Come in," Reagan said as she put her phone down. Once she saw that it was Laura, she said, "Hey, Joe, let me call you back in a little bit. I'll let you know when my flight is supposed to land. Okay, bye."

"Going somewhere?" she asked walking into the room.

"Listen, Laura, I appreciate your hospitality and all, but me and Jewel were only supposed to be on our honeymoon for two weeks. Today marks two weeks, and he still has no idea when he wants to go home. I know that it may be easy for him to forget because he's caught up in the moment right now, but we have children to take care of."

"It looks like you have your mind made up, huh?" she asked looking down at her half-filled suitcase.

"Yes," Reagan said looking down.

"Maybe it's for the best then."

"What is?"

"You leaving," Laura began, "My son is a very special man, and I'm not sure that you understand that. He has responsibilities that he is destined to carry out for our family, but he is hesitant because he is afraid of what you will think of him. You have tried to force him to be this person he was never intended to be. He's not fulfilled in life, Reagan, and I'm afraid that you may be holding him back."

"Holding him back?" she asked offended, "I have always been by Jewel's side. No, I don't want him selling drugs for his family or anyone else, but don't accuse me of not supporting him. I want nothing but the best for Jewel."

"If that's true, Reagan, then you will leave him alone. Can't you see the light that has returned in him? The only other time I can remember him smiling so much was when he was a child."

"That's probably because you haven't been there since he was a child."

"But I'm here now, and I will be the one to usher my son into greatness. His rightful place is here with his family, and if you cannot be supportive of that, then it would be in your best interest to just disappear. The children will be taken care of though; I assure you," Laura said pulling a cigarette from out of her pocketbook before lighting the tip.

"Is that a threat?"

"Think of it more as a suggestion," she said getting up to leave, "Think about it."

$$$$$

"Mom, Mom," Jewel said busting into her room as the darkness immediately swallowed him.

"What is it, Jewel?" Laura asked jumping up out of her sleep. She quickly tried to turn on the light struggling to see the clock that read *4:06 a.m.*

"Have you seen, Reagan? She's not in her room, and all of her stuff is gone."

They had been avoiding each other the entire night, but after sleeping in separate rooms for a few hours, he began to miss the warmth of her flesh. He swallowed his pride and went to say his sorries, but she was nowhere to be found. The only thing in her place was a note on the nightstand.

Jewel,

After thinking about everything, I decided to go home. I am so glad that you are able to reconnect with your family, but I think that this is something you need to do on your own. I hope that you finally find what you're looking for.

-Reagan

"All I found was a note," he said in frustration. He had been trying to call her ever since he read the last word, but she never picked up. "When you talked to her, did she say anything?" He was desperate for any understanding. Reagan had been so hot and cold lately that it was getting harder and harder to figure her out.

"She seemed fine when we talked. She had just gotten off the phone with the baby."

"So what did you say to her?"

"I explained the importance of you coming to work for the family. She said she understood how much this meant to you, and she just wants you to be happy."

"She said that?"

"Yes."

"How can I be happy without my family?" he asked as he balled up the small sheet of white paper and threw it at the door.

"Don't think of it like that, Jewel. With your talent, you will ensure that your great great great great great grandkids will never have to work a day in their lives. Maybe a little space will be good for you two. You need room to let your wings spread."

"I don't know, Mom. Reagan is a big part of my life. I need her to be okay with this."

"And she will be, Jewel. I promise you," she said placing his face in between her hands, "Once she sees you in your element, she will see that happy person she fell in love with. You have been so miserable, son. Now it's time to live the life you're supposed to live. While there are greater risks in this job, there are even greater rewards, and you don't have to worry about worthless punks like Kisino Brown."

Although, he wanted Reagan's approval, deep down, he wanted to continue the work Golden died for even more. With his mother's offer, he would be able to ensure that he and his potnahs could eat forever. Looking at the bigger picture, Jewel knew that he would be an idiot if he didn't take accept.

"Okay," he said as his chest filled with excitement.

"Is that a yes?"

"Yes, but only on the condition that my niggas are a part of this every step of the way."

"All I can guarantee is that they get the chance to meet with your grandfather. He makes all the shots."

"That's more than enough," Jewel said getting up to leave the room, "Call Grandpa Joseph and tell him I'm ready. D.R., here we come."

$$$$$

The Next Morning...

Jewel woke up in an empty bed and couldn't help but miss Reagan. He hated how he always had to pick his family over his career when he dedicated himself to both. After fifty missed calls and ten voicemails, he finally realized that she needed to be alone for a while. He hated feeling like the bad guy in the situation, but no matter what he chose, he was going to lose. After spending a few extra days in Barbados, Smackz and Stevin decided to head back to the States. Needing to finalize their transfer of responsibility to Jewel, Laura rode with them to the airport. She needed to confirm a few last minute details before their trip. Left alone to his own devices, Jewel used the time to sit out and enjoy the island breeze. The hot tropical sun showered down on his deep caramel-colored skin as he laid by the pool, but he soon got bored without the sweet sound of Reagan's voice to annoy him. Wanting to take his mind off of his marital issues, he called Sacario.

"What's up, bwoy? You still out in Barbados?"

"Yep, you know just living this island life."

"When you coming back?"

"Soon. Reagan decided to skate on a nigga, so you know I can't stay."

"What?"

"Yep, she left sometime last night. She wrote a note saying that she hopes I find what I'm looking for. Whatever the fuck that means."

"She probably was just missing lil man, bruh. I know how Kiko gets about Ari. She doesn't let this little girl go anywhere without her let alone leave her somewhere for a few weeks."

"Naw, it's more than that. I think she's upset about this proposition I got from my mom."

"What proposition? I know ya'll just reconnected, but she giving niggas jobs already?"

"It's bigger than that. She's distro, blood."

"What?"

"All the work that Golden got, kept, stored, sold, whatever came from her or my grandfather I should say."

"Are you serious? That's huge for M.A.C."

"Who you telling? But there's more."

"What's more than that?"

"She wants me to step in. We would control the M.A.C. Boys entire distribution network along with others across the country."

"We?"

"Smackz is going to take over the day-to-day operations, and I want you and K-2 to come work with me."

"Jewel, if you're messing with me, I'm fucking you up."

"Nigga, you can try," he said laughing, "but you know I never play when it comes to money."

"So what does this mean?"

"Nothing is final yet. I still have to meet up with my dad's dad, but if everything goes according to plan, no more small timing. Our families will be set for life out here swimming in these clear blue waters."

"You know I'm in. That goes without saying. This is what I've wanted. Not the plug shit, but you finally coming back into yourself. You were lost, bruh, but you've never sounded more like yourself than you do right now."

"I've tried that top to bottom shit, and it doesn't work for me. I don't want my boys working for me. I want ya'll to work with me, and this is the perfect way to do that."

"Like I said, I'm coming for sure, but I don't know about K with the baby coming and all."

"Just put it in his ear. There's no way he'll turn down an opportunity like this. Him, Gabby, and the baby will be sitting on a hill somewhere."

"What you need from me?"

"I'ma call you back with all the details, but get ready to fly out here."

"Yep."

"One," Jewel said hanging up.

"Who was that?" Kiko asked being nosey as she snuck up behind Sacario.

"Jewel."

"How's the honeymoon going?"

"They didn't go on a honeymoon. They went to Barbados to visit his mom. Well, he did. Reagan ended up coming home early or something."

"By herself?"

"You know how ya'll get."

"Don't do that," she said rolling her eyes, "Everything a woman does cannot always be blamed on her period."

"Look, I didn't ask him too much about it. She probably just missed her son, and Jewel is out there on business. Speaking of, I need to go holla at K. We got some big things coming, baby," he said kissing her on the lips before grabbing his coat, "I'll be back, later," and that quick, he was out the door.

$$\$\$\$\$$$

After a two hour drive, Hassan found himself in front of Diamond's apartment. He checked his freshly cut line and facial hair in the rearview mirror before he grabbed the two dozen deep dark blue, purple, and pink roses that sat on the leather passenger seat.

"Hey, I'm outside," he said answering his phone as he walked toward her gate.

"Stay right there. I'm on my way down now."

"Damn, you don't want me to see where you live?"

"This is our first date, Hassan. You're acting a little presumptuous."

"My bad," he said wanting to respect her boundaries, "I'm where I was parked last time."

"Here I come," she said hanging up.

He fixed his jacket and tie in his reflection as he waited. He never dressed so formally for a date before, but he had something special planned for the night. As he waited, his phone rang again. This time it was Sacario.

"What's up, blood? Where you at with it? I drove past your house, but I didn't see your car."

"You should've called me earlier. I'm out the way now. What's up though?"

"Please don't tell me this has anything to do with Diamond?"

"Man, what's up?"

"Listen, I talked to Jewel earlier, and he has a move that can really put the M.A.C. Boys on the map. I don't wanna say too much, but we need to be in Barbados like yesterday."

"So when we going?"

"I'm just waiting to hear back from Jewel. Once he hits me, I'll let you know."

"Yep," Hassan said hanging up the phone.

A few moments later, he heard the large, iron gate slam shut. When he looked up, he saw Diamond coming toward him in an all-white, almost sheer gown. Her crystal encrusted pumps glittered under the moonlight illuminating every step she took. Hassan was breathless. She looked like a goddess.

"Why'd I have to get so dressed up? Where are we going?"

"It's a surprise," he said opening the car door for her, "These are for you by the way." His hand shook as he handed her the bouquet of his affections.

"They're beautiful, Hassan. Thank you," she said kissing him on the cheek before getting in, "You know I'm not used to all this."

"Used to all what?" He hurried to walk back around to his side.

"All this."

"Let you tell it, and you got nothing but niggas tricking on you," he said turning the car on.

"It's not the same. A dude can always buy you something. It's the little things that count, you know?"

"You deserve it," he said looking over at her before pulling out in traffic.

Twenty minutes later, they arrived at the river. Hassan parked alongside a fleet of large boats that glowed against the water.

"What's all this?"

"Well, despite what you may think, I think you're a very sophisticated and sexy woman, and I know that you've probably been to a million and one restaurants before, so I thought that we would have dinner on the water tonight."

"I have to say I am very impressed," Diamond said unable to keep herself from cheesing, "No one has ever put this much effort in for me. Thank you."

"Hello, there," a hostess said as they neared the dock, "Welcome to the Nightingale. Do you have reservations for tonight?"

"Actually, I reserved this particular boat for the evening. It should be under Williams."

"Oh, yes, so sorry, Mr. Williams. Right this way." She led them aboard and into the private dining room that awaited. Diamond appreciated the peace and quiet.

"I still can't believe you did all this for me," she said admiring the candle-lit interior.

"I want you to know how serious I am about you, Diamond. I know that everybody's been trying to give me the red light about you, but I see something I like, and I want to get to know you better. I don't find too many females I gel with, you know?"

"Sorry to interrupt, but the captain asked me to see if you would like to have dinner outside on the deck? Since we won't be having any other guests tonight, it would be a much more romantic option."

"Yeah, that sounds nice," Hassan said.

"Perfect, here are two complimentary glasses of our house champagne. Go up the stairs there to your right, and our staff will take care of everything else. Enjoy."

Hassan led Diamond up and outside to the deck. The dark blue water rippled under the boat as it slowly drifted away from the dock, but the moon and stars maintained their reflection below.

"This is beautiful," she said leaning over the balcony.

"Yeah, it's nice out tonight. It's a little cold though. You want my jacket?"

"No, I'm good. You keep it," she said rubbing her arms.

"Don't be ridiculous. Take it." Not taking no for an answer, he draped it over her shoulders.

"Thank you," she said looking up into his eyes.

"Did I tell you how beautiful you look tonight?"

"No, but you can now." She leaned in to kiss him, but he quickly backed away. "I'm sorry. I just thought...," she said finally looking up, "You're the first guy that I've felt comfortable around since Jewel."

"I'm glad, ma," he said stroking the side of her cheek, "But I gotta do this right."

"What do you mean?"

"Me and Sacario are going to go handle some business with Jewel in the next few days, and I'm gonna ask for his permission to really approach you how you deserve. I like you, but I can't let that jeopardize what I have going on with Sacario. That's like my brother, so it's a respect thing, you know? I have to make sure Jewel's okay with it first."

"So what are you gonna say?"

"I don't know yet, but being that you're the mother of his child, I just feel like a conversation needs to be had."

"What if he's not fucking with it?"

"Is that what you want?"

"At this point, no. I know that I was holding onto Jewel because I felt like he was the only one who could turn me back into the person I was before I met Marcus. I wanted to go back to when things were normal, and I had it in my head that he could give that back to me. I know he doesn't love me. He hasn't in a very long time."

"I don't know what this nigga's gonna say, but let's not even worry about all that right now. You're here with me," he said pulling her closer to him by her waist. Diamond laid her head on his shoulders as they stared out over the water into the stars forgetting about everything but each other for the rest of the night.

Chapter 10

After another exhausting trip across the country, all Reagan wanted was her son. She and Joe agreed that she would wait until the morning, but she couldn't. Chase was one of the only things she had that was normal in her life, and she would do whatever she had to do to hold onto that.

Knock. Knock. Knock.

"Reagan, baby, what are you doing here?" Isabella asked quickly opening the door.

"Sorry, it's so late, Ms. Izzy. I knew I was gonna miss Chase when I got home, so I had to come get my baby. Did I wake you?"

"Actually, no, we were just on our way out. Let me go get Joe. Come in."

Reagan walked inside excited to see the familiar.

"Hey, Rea, I thought you were coming in the morning?" he asked walking down the stairs.

"I was, but I missed my baby," she said poking her lips out.

"He was sleeping, but Isabella is getting his stuff together now," he said sitting down on the couch, "so Jewel really didn't come back, huh? I can't believe it."

"I can," she said shaking her head, "I knew it was only a matter of time. I mean how could he resist with Laura promising him the keys to the kingdom?"

"What do you mean?" he asked making sure Isabella was still upstairs.

"The same day we got there, she told Jewel that she wanted him back in the family business." Joe stared down at the floor. "Did you know about Golden?"

"Of course, he was my wife's brother, but by the time I found out that Jewel had been so integrated into that life, it was too late. I wasn't against him getting to know his uncle. I was just against Golden using my son like a drug mule."

"Well, he's definitely back at it. I know Pop's death really sent him over the edge, but I never thought that this was what he needed."

"I gave him a bath earlier, and he already ate dinner, so you can just stick him right back into bed once you guys get home," Isabella said walking back down the stairs.

"I wish there was some way you could talk some sense into him," Reagan said getting up to grab Chase from her arms.

"Some sense into who?"

"No one, honey," he said wrapping his arms around her shoulders.

"Thank you guys so much again. I know he's a handful," she said grabbing Chase's bag.

"It's always a pleasure, Reagan. Don't be a stranger, okay?"

"I won't. See you guys later." She walked outside to her car as she pulled Chase's hood over his head trying to protect him from the midnight breeze.

After leaving Joe and Isabella's, all she wanted to do was get in her bed. She didn't know where she stood with Jewel, but she didn't want to think about it anymore. When she pulled in the driveway, an unknown car was parked out front. She was already on edge, so she watched the car for a few minutes before getting out. She hurried to grab Chase and his bag and quickly walked toward the front door.

"Reagan? Reagan?" she heard someone say behind her.

"Kiko?" she asked turning around peering through the darkness, "What are you doing here?"

"I'm so sorry to just pop up like this. I didn't have your number," she said walking closer. Reagan could see that she had her daughter nestled against her neck as well. "Sacario told me that you came back from Barbados...without Jewel. I just wanted to make sure you were okay."

"I really appreciate that," she said opening up the front door, "Come in."

"After everything that happened before you guys left, and then this, I thought you might need someone to talk to."

"Thanks," Reagan said not knowing how to read her. As much as she missed Robyn, she was now convinced that females couldn't be trusted. She grew up with Robyn, and they were close enough to be sisters, but that didn't stop her from stabbing Reagan in the back every chance she got. And even though she was thankful that Diamond was there when she almost lost Chase, she always knew that she was using her to get to Jewel. She wanted to give her the benefit of the doubt, but of course she wasn't surprised when Diamond confessed her undying love. She didn't really know Kiko, but she couldn't be much different, right?

"You can lay Arianna down in here," she said turning on the light in Chase's room, "I'm surprised Sacario isn't with you."

"He doesn't know I'm here," she admitted, "He wouldn't understand, you know?"

"Understand what?"

"What's it's like to be with guys like him and Jewel. Females only see the money and the status, and they think that's life. They don't know about the late nights we spend waiting to see if they make it back home, or being afraid to answer the phone when they're not with you because you don't ever wanna get that call. It's rough."

"Tell me about it."

After making sure the kids were snuggled in bed, Kiko and Reagan went back downstairs into the living room.

"You want something to drink?"

"Do you have any wine?"

"Yeah, we should," Reagan said walking into the kitchen over to their wine rack. She pulled the last bottle of chardonnay they had left and grabbed a glass from the cabinet.

Well, I guess I won't be seeing you for a while, she thought staring down at the olive-colored bottle as she popped the cork.

"When I came over here with Sacario that night, I was a little standoffish," Kiko said sitting down.

"Really?" Reagan said laughing as she passed her the glass.

"It had nothing to do with you though. I could just tell that Diamond was fake as fuck, but it seemed like you two were close. I try not to be messy, you know?"

"I know how it looked to everybody, but to me, our sons are brothers. No, they don't share the same blood, but they still have Jewel in common. After everything that she had been through, I felt connected to that, so it was easy for me to let her in. She needed a friend, and I wanted to be that. Shit, I think I needed one too, but at the end of the day, a bitch will always show her true colors."

"Have you talked to her lately?"

"For what? I have enough going on with Jewel to be worrying about Diamond's drama."

"Speaking of, I don't want to get in your business or anything, but what happened? Sacario told me that he's supposed to be flying out to Barbados in the next few days to link up with him."

And it starts. "Before our wedding, Jewel's mom showed up and left her information to have him call her. He has spent almost his whole life hating his parents because he feels like they abandoned him, and rightfully so. By the grace of God, Jewel was able to repair his relationship with Joe, so when Laura showed up, I knew that he at least wanted to hear her out."

"That's a good thing, right? I mean he probably wants to try and fix things with his mom too."

"At Pop's funeral, Jewel vowed to me that he was done with the game. I think the weight of the situation got to him. He already went to sit down for like six-months for some bullshit, so he knew that if he continued, either that would be his future or being laid up somewhere in a body bag. I want nothing but the best for Jewel, and that includes his safety, so I can't lie and say that when he told me that he was done, it wasn't music to my ears, but over this past year, he hasn't been himself, you know? He kinda just floated through the world with no purpose. It was like all of the life had been sucked out of him, so believe me, I was gung-ho when his mother reached out. I felt like maybe she was the missing piece he needed. Maybe she could fix him, but I was wrong."

"Well, being that Sacario is now involved, I can't say that Jewel is still keeping his hands clean."

"We were in Barbados for two weeks, and during that time, he found out anything and everything he didn't know about his family. Golden being his uncle was only one of them. That was like the spark he needed or something. After Laura told him that, I don't think he saw anything other than the M.A.C. Boys, not even me, Chase, or Jailen."

"Stop thinking of it like that," Kiko said refilling her empty wine glass, "Do you think that I would've chosen this life for Sacario if I had the choice? I really wish that he would've went off to college with Hassan and explored his options outside of the Bay, but this is what he wanted. Golden has been a part of my family for years, and I could never repay him for all the stuff he helped me and Sacario with. He helped create the man he is today, and those same values, thank God, were passed down to my brother Keith. Golden was a standup man. He may have done things a little differently, but his heart was always in it, and I know that Jewel is a good man too. The M.A.C. Boys mean more to them than we could ever understand. They really look at each other like family, and for a lot of them, it was the first, shit, maybe even the only one they've ever been a part of. It's sacred, and they will do anything to hold onto it. If this is what breaks you and Jewel up for good, I can't say too much because I don't know you guys'

Sasha Ravae

relationship, but from the outside looking in, he adores you. You have to understand that some people are police officers, lawyers, politicians, while others happen to sell drugs. It may not be right, but there's a little dirt in all of them. You may not like what he does, but you and Jewel are married now. It's for better or worse, baby," Kiko said taking a sip.

"I love him. I could never question that, but I don't know if I have it in me to go through all this shit again. I was alone my entire pregnancy. I don't want to go through the same thing with this one," Reagan said looking down and rubbing her belly.

"Oh my gosh, you're pregnant?" she asked setting her glass down.

"Barely. I can't be more than a few weeks."

"Congratulations, girl." Kiko got up to give her a hug. "I was wondering why you weren't drinking. You had me over here feeling like a lush."

"I took a pregnancy test in Barbados."

"I know Jewel is excited. I hope you guys have a little girl. She would be beautiful," she said having baby fever herself.

"J doesn't know."

"What? Why not?"

"We had been going at it the entire trip, so it never came up."

"That's why you've been tripping. Those pregnancy hormones ain't no joke."

"I don't know..."

"Listen, you love Jewel, and he worships the ground you walk on. Sometimes you just have to work with your man, and this may be one of those times. You better get to working before you have more to worry about than just Diamond."

$$$$$

Beeeeeeeeeeeeeeep.

K-2's shop door sounded as Sacario made his way inside.

"I'm glad I caught you before you cut, blood," he said giving him a hug.

"You almost missed me, bruh."

"What you doing here so late?"

"I had a last minute client," K-2 said hurrying to finish cleaning up his station, "Where's K at?"

"In Sac," Sacario said shaking his head.

120

"What the fuck is she doing out there so late?"

"With Reagan Sanchez surprisingly. I don't know if I should be worried or not."

"That's what you wanted, right? I've been telling her for years that she needs some new friends. The hoes she runs with now are tired," he laughed, "Believe me."

"I guess," Sacario said sitting down.

"Don't do her like that. Reagan's solid. I'm glad K's getting out more."

"She's on her way back now. I called her as soon as you told me Gabrielle's water broke."

"Man, I'm so juiced, my nigga. Joe and Isabella should on their way here now. Gabby will flip the fuck out if I show up without her mama," K-2 said looking down at this phone, "but my bad, blood, what did you need to talk to me about?"

"So you know how Jewel's mom showed up and let him know that Golden was really his uncle, right?"

"Yeah, I mean if you think about it, he was super protective over Jewel. He laid Brandon's ass out flat, no questions asked."

"Well, apparently since G is gone, it's been decided that Smackz will step in as number one."

"Decided by who?" K-2 asked finally looking up from his phone. "By the plug, bruh."

"And who is that?" He knew how hard Sacario had worked to climb his way up the ladder, and he deserved everything that came to him. He didn't want to see him have to start over from square one.

"Jewel's mom and his other uncle Stevin."

"Wait, what?" he asked adjusting his fitted cap.

"G was being plugged by Jewel's family the entire time. That's why he saw so much bread."

"If Smackz is taking over the M.A.C. Boys, where does that leave you?"

"That's the real reason I'm here. Jewel's mom put it to him like she and his uncle are ready to sit down and enjoy the fruits of their labor, and she wants him to take over her position."

"Wow, that's big."

"That not it though. He want us to come with him." K-2 remained quiet. "I'm not a hundred-percent on all the details yet, but it's Jewel. This is what we've been waiting for, K. We'll finally have the opportunity to align the M.A.C. Boys right where we need to be. There's nothing stopping us now. Jewel wants us to fly out to Barbados in the next couple of days to have a meeting with his grandfather. I guess that's where the work really comes from."

"As much as I appreciate you thinking about me, I can't say yes to that, Cari. My fiancée is about to give birth to my first born. There's not enough money in the world to make me miss that. Jewel has M.A.C. in his blood, so it's not surprising that he's taking advantage of this opportunity, but I'm so thankful for him leaving when he did. I began to look at life differently, and my priorities changed. All that is important to me now is being a good man who my wife and daughter can be proud of and to take care of them the best way I can. Business is popping, my nigga. I might fuck around and have a chain of these mothafuckas," K-2 said admiring his hard work.

"You sure, K? With this move, we will be set for life. You won't have to work anymore."

"Yeah, I'm sure. Like I said, some things are more important that money. I'll be around though, blood. It ain't like I'm dead or nothing."

"It's not gon' be the same without you," Sacario said dropping his head.

"Don't start crying," K-2 laughed, "Your niece is about to enter the world. There's a lot for us to be happy about right now, and plus, I'll see you. You are married to my sister."

"I know we're fam and all, but that's not the problem. It's just we've been thugging since I can remember."

"Well, it's time for me to do something different now. Say what's up to Jewel for me, and tell him he better do shit right this time. He got a lot riding on it."

"Kiss the baby for me," Sacario said getting up to leave. He hurried outside before K-2 could see the tears that were beginning to well up in his eyes. He had been around him since he was young, but he was proud of the man K-2 had become. They clicked because they both were addicted to the street life, but K-2 had elevated himself to want so much more.

Beeeeeeeeeeeeeeep.

$$$$$

Three Days Later…

Ever since Diamond and Hassan had their first date, they became inseparable. He had been coming out to Sac to see her, but this time, she offered to drive down to Richmond. She had to admit that she was really starting to like him, so she was excited to take the trip. She didn't know if Hassan was just a rebound, but she appreciated the distraction from Jewel. Although she tried to fight it, she craved the familiar, but the feeling was always one-sided. She was scared to start over again because of how things turned out with Marcus, but everything in her being was screaming that Hassan was different.

An hour and a half later, Diamond pulled up in front of his house. She immediately spotted his Lexus, but she didn't recognize the silver Infinite that sat hectically behind it. After parking, she checked her makeup in the rearview mirror before putting on one more coat of M.A.C. Viva Glam II and getting out of the car. Butterflies filled her stomach with each step she took as she made her way to the front door. She let out a deep breath before knocking, but she soon noticed that the door was already open. She walked in but didn't see Hassan anywhere. She thought he wasn't home until she heard him yelling from upstairs. She couldn't tell who he was talking to, but she made her way up the steps anyway. When she reached the top, she could see into his bedroom. His things were thrown everywhere, and as she got closer, she could see the deep scratches that covered his face and chest.

"So this must be the bitch?" Chyna asked snapping her neck toward the door as her 26" Mongolian extensions fell in her face.

"Diamond, baby, I can explain," he said looking like he had just been caught red-handed.

"Baby? Forreal, Hassan?" Chyna said rolling her eyes.

"Oh, so you don't fuck with her, huh? I knew you were full of shit," Diamond said turning around to leave, "This must be why you never wanted me to come out here." She hurried down the stairs disgusted that she had let her guard down.

"When I get back, you better be the fuck out of my house," he barked at Chyna before he ran after her.

By the time he got outside, she was already in her car pulling out of the driveway. Not willing to risk her leaving and never speaking to him again, he ran in the middle of the street praying she didn't hit him.

"Hassan, move before I run your ass over," Diamond yelled out of the window.

"Not until you let me explain."

"Let you explain what? How you're a manipulator and a liar just like the rest of these niggas? If you still fuck with the bitch, why couldn't you just tell me that? I told you everything about my situation. Why'd you have to pull that 'ol, 'it's only you, baby' bullshit?"

"Diamond, I never lied. It is only you."

"Explain that bitch then cause I bet you she would say otherwise."

"When I got home from the gym, Chyna was there. She said she left some shit here. I knew she was lying, but I entertained the stupid bitch anyway. Not even five minutes after, she was questioning me about you. She said that one of her potnahs saw this picture of you I posted on IG…"

"You posted a picture of me?" Diamond asked smiling a little.

"Just something I took that night we had dinner," he smiled back, "but I mean I was honest with her. I told her that I'm interested in being with you, and that's when she lost it. She went 51/50 forreal. I tried to grab her, but she started scratching me with those fucking devil nails. Why do females get those anyway?"

"Fuck you, nigga. This shit isn't over," Chyna spat with her heels in her hand as she walked out of the house, "For you either, bitch." She jumped in her car and backed out so fast that she almost hit them.

After the smoke cleared, he continued, "Look, I know I got myself out here looking like an asshole, but you gotta believe that I'm not lying about this. Did you just see that bitch? Why would I want that when I could have you? My dream girl," he said walking around to her side, "Diamond Christine White, I like you."

"I don't know if I can be with somebody who has bitches out here in the world acting like lunatics. What other crazy hoe do you have waiting on the sidelines?"

"I just want you," he said opening her door and bending down to kiss her, "I don't want to have to sneak around with you. I want us to be together, and when I want something, it's hard for me to hear no. Can you come inside please? I just want to talk to you."

"Okay," she said kissing him back. He had made it clear and apparent what his intentions were, and just for the moment, Diamond was all in. Sparks shot through her body as his soft lips touched hers. She melted into him until she felt like she was floating. For the first time in a long time, she felt at home.

"Let me get out of the street," Hassan said breaking their embrace, "Park right behind me." He walked back up the driveway and waited for her by the door.

"I shouldn't even be in here after all this bullshit," she said disgusted as she crossed her arms across her chest and walked back inside.

"It's not like I fucked her," he laughed. Diamond instantly cut him with her eyes. "Too soon?"

"Too soon."

"I'm sorry," he said slowly wrapping his arms around her thick hips, "It ain't like I didn't know you were coming or something. You act like you caught a nigga creeping. When I got home and saw that bitch in my bed, the first thing I thought about was you. I know how it looked, but you have no idea how hard I was tryna get her ass out."

"Sssshhhh," she said kissing him again. She knew that their situation was complicated, but that didn't stop her from wanting him. Jewel made his feelings for her known long before, and at first, Diamond wasn't ready to let him go, but now, she done fighting.

She wrestled with Hassan's belt as she left a trail of wet kisses along the side of his neck. "Diamond, we don't have to do this," he moaned as she caressed his chest, "I was serious when I said I wanted to talk."

"You sure?" she asked looking down. His dick fought to break out of his boxers with each touch of her lips against his smooth brown skin.

Not needing to be asked twice, Hassan led her into the guest bedroom and laid her down on the freshly made bed.

"Damn, I've been waiting to do this ever since I first saw you," he said taking off his shirt, "You looked like a queen in that all-white. I tried my best to be respectful, baby, but you made it so hard."

He pulled her sundress up and laid kisses from her belly button down both of her thighs.

"Oooohhh, Hassan, that feels so good," she said letting low moans escape.

"Can I taste it?"

Diamond slipped off her black thong and he was face-to-face with her kitty. He softly kissed it sending chills up her spine. She arched her back, and he went in head first. He cupped her pearl with his tongue and her juices covered his lips. She pulled her dress up and over her head and played with her titties as he continued to feast. He spread her thighs open as far as they could go and began to fuck her with his tongue. Diamond felt herself coming. He sucked her pussy until her body felt weak, but he didn't stop. He put his two fingers in his mouth until they were both wet, and then he slowly stroked her insides. She grinded against his hand letting her head fall back in ecstasy.

"Fuck, baby, that pussy is so wet," he said tasting her satisfaction off his fingers.

"I want you, Sani," she said unable to take anymore.

He pulled his wallet out of his pants' pocket and found the condom that was still inside. As his dick stuck straight out, he quickly unraveled the latex across his anticipation. Diamond scooted up to the top of the bed. It had been a while since she last had sex. She practically felt like a virgin again, but Hassan knew that. There was no need to rush. They had all the time in the world, so he took it. He showered her body with kisses before coming back up and twirling his tongue around her nipples as he gently played with her pussy. Diamond grabbed his dick and rubbed it around her clit. Hassan's hot, wet skin pressing against hers turned her on. He continued to rub his dick against her clit down to her hole before she slowly guided him inside. He could feel her walls stretch as he slowly opened her up.

"You okay?" he asked kissing her on the lips, "I can go slower if you want."

"No, you're fine," she said enjoying his touch. Finding his rhythm, she began to relax and fell into the moment. Hassan was everything she needed and more.

After forty-five minutes of body exploration, Diamond laid on his sweaty chest as he put one in the air.

"Now I get it," she said snuggling him a little tighter as her pussy pulsated.

"Get what?" he asked as he hit the blunt.

"Why that girl was in here acting crazy like that," she said looking up at him.

"And why is that?" he smiled.

"Dick too bomb," Diamond sang.

"I mean..."

"I'm just kidding...well, not really," she laughed, "I guess I just mean that it was nice. I haven't had sex in over a year, and I know we kinda just met, but..."

"But nothing. If I was just trying to fuck you, I would've tried the first night I met you. I'm serious about this us thing. I know it's new, but for me, it feels right."

"It feels right for me too," she said kissing him on the neck, "but you keep talking about us being together. How do you propose we really do that though?" Her feelings for Hassan were definitely starting to grow.

"Come to Barbados with me."

"What?"

"I told you that Sacario has some business to handle with Jewel, and he wants me to come too," he said looking in her eyes.

"What about Jewel?"

"Like I said, I'm gonna talk to him. I'ma put it all out there. I like you, Diamond, and I don't care who knows it."

"I like you too, Hassan, and that's saying a lot coming from me, but I don't need Jewel's approval anymore. He doesn't run my life, and he's made it more than clear that he doesn't want to be with me anymore. If I found someone who makes me happy, I shouldn't have to run it by him first."

"It's not about that, Diamond. Jewel is in the same circle I am, and after this trip, that circle could get even smaller. It's only right to let him know what's going on between me and you."

"Whatever you gotta do to make you feel comfortable in this situation, I want you to do it, but me and Jewel under one roof is always a disaster. As much as I would like to go, I can't in good conscience. I don't want to be the focal point of all this drama surrounding me anymore. I just want to be happy."

"I don't know how long I'ma be gone."

"I'm not going anywhere."

"Is there anything I can do to change your mind?"

She shook her head no. "That last time was it for me and Jewel. I'm ready to put the past behind me and move forward for the sake of our son. Have this conversation for you, baby," Diamond said sitting up, "but like I said, I'ma be right here waiting for you."

Chapter 11

"Jewel's mama is out here living the life, my nigga," Hassan said staring out of the car window as they drove to meet him.

"Yeah, they living in paradise, blood," Sacario said inhaling the fresh island air. After Kiko had their daughter, it had been a while since he'd been on vacation.

"So what's the plan?"

"Jewel said that we're flying out to the Dominican Republic to meet with his grandfather tonight, and if everything goes according to plan, we'll be in business by the morning, bruh."

"This is like an interview or something?"

"I don't think nothing as formal as that. You gotta think Jewel didn't fuck with any of his family before this, so it's not like he can just go in there on the strength of his relationship with grandfather. We're all gonna be in there proving ourselves."

"I'm with it," Hassan said sitting straight up, "I just gotta do one thing first."

"Do what?"

"I just need to talk to him about something. That's all."

"Something like what?"

"You ain't gon' stop, huh?"

"You know me too well, bruh."

"I need to holla at him about Diamond."

"About who?" Sacario asked shaking his head, "Man, I knew you was still messing with her. You've been M.I.A. ever since you met her. Please tell me that you're just gonna tell him that it was a one-time thing, but now it's done. This is about business, Sani, and I'm not letting anything get in the way of that."

"Cari, blood, it wasn't just a one-time thing. Like I told you, I'm feeling lil baby, and I'm tryna see where it goes. Being that I'm not tryna have any problems, as a man, I feel like I gotta let him know what's up. I don't plan on missing out on this money, but I'm not willing to let her go either."

"Okay, now I know you fucked."

"Here you go," Hassan said sitting back and throwing his hands in the air.

"In my opinion, this is bad for business, bruh, but if you're adamant about letting this nigga know that you're fucking his baby mama, can you at least do it another time? I'm not tryna have nothing make this go left right now."

"Have I ever let you down?"

"Man, it's not about that..."

"Have I?" he repeated

Sacario thought over their friendship, and Hassan had always been solid. He didn't want to start second-guessing his judgment now.

"Naw."

"You gotta trust me then."

$$$$$

Jewel woke up ready to face the world, but there was still something missing. Reagan had been gone for a few days. Every day he called in to check on her and Chase, but she never answered. Luckily, Joe called him when she came to his house, but he didn't say too much about their visit.

"Reagan, this is like the hundredth time I've tried to call you. We need to talk," he sighed into the phone as he rubbed his eyes, "I know that you don't understand this right now, but I need you. Please don't give up on me, baby."

"She's still not picking up?" Laura asked walking into the room.

"Naw, but I know if I could just talk to her, I..."

"Jewel, maybe this is for the best," she said sitting down in the chair next to him.

"How do you figure?"

"Reagan's a very sweet girl, don't get me wrong, but she is not cut out to be with a man like you. You have a great responsibility to this family, Jewel, and I just see her as a distraction for you."

"You don't know her like I do," he said wanting to believe in his wife.

"If I remember correctly, didn't she have a relationship with your little friend Brandon Edwards?"

"Mom, I know how it looks from the outside looking in, but things were complicated back then. We're not the same people."

"No, she is the complication, Jewel. Your life could really be so much simpler."

"We're married now. We're not on some boyfriend/girlfriend shit."

"Yeah, so were your father and I, and you see how that turned out."

Ding. Dong.

"I got it," he said getting up not wanting to talk about Reagan anymore, "That's probably Sacario and K-2."

"Well, you boys meet me in the dining hall for breakfast. Ana should be finishing up now."

Jewel ran downstairs to answer the door. "I got it," he said beating Kurt to the front. When he opened it, their driver was bringing Sacario and Hassan's bags up the steps.

"What's up, nigga?" Sacario asked with a smile plastered across his face.

"How was your flight?" Jewel walked outside into the heat as the sun kissed his already tanned skin.

"It was cool. Long as fuck, but it was cool," Sacario said giving him a hug, "You remember Hassan, right?"

"Yeah, what's up, bruh? How you doing?"

"Cool."

"Where's K-2 at?"

"About that," Sacario said walking inside, "He's not coming."

"Not coming? Why not?"

"First, Gabby had the baby..."

"Forreal? Fuck, I gotta call her. I just talked to my pops too, and he didn't even say anything. He's flying out here later then?"

"Naw, bruh...he's done."

"Done?"

"Yeah, he said that he's really serious about that barber shit. He's done."

"I can't do anything but respect it. My sister deserves that, you know?"

Jewel was proud of K-2. He had grown up so much that he envied the man he had become. He wished that it would have been easy for him to let the game go too. He wished Pop would've taken his way out when he had the chance, but just like him, he couldn't let the streets go either.

"Well, don't just stand there in front of the door, Jewel," Laura said walking out into the foyer, "You all come on in. Breakfast is ready."

"Mom, this is Sacario James and Hassan Williams. They flew out from Richmond."

"Very nice to meet you both," she said shaking their hands, "Kurt, take their bags upstairs please. Put them in the junior suites."

"Thank you, Mrs. Sanchez, for your hospitality. Your place is very beautiful," Sacario said as they walked into the dining hall.

"Laura will do," she smiled, "And thank you. This place has been in our family for many years now. Can I get either of you something to drink?"

"What would you recommend? This is our first time to the islands," Hassan said sitting down at the table.

"The rum punch of course," she laughed, "It's never too early for rum punch."

"Rum punch it is then," Sacario said sitting down beside Hassan.

"Ana," she yelled over her shoulder.

"Yes, madam."

"We are ready to start."

"Perfect," she said standing at the head of the table, "This morning, I have prepared for you scrambled eggs with honey roasted ham, fried flying fish, sautéed sweet potatoes with onions, peppers, and chives, fried plantains, and to complete the meal, cinnamon dusted pumpkin fritters."

"That sounds amazing," Sacario said as he listened to his stomach rumble.

"And we'll also get started with a round of punch," Laura said placing the oversized white cloth napkin that sat next to her onto her lap.

"Of course, madam."

"While we wait, why don't we take this time to formally introduce ourselves," she said turning to face Sacario.

"Okay, ummmm, I guess I'll go first. Like Jewel, I have been in the M.A.C. Boys since I was a teenager. Golden was a very influential person in my life. Because of him, I have what I have today. All the flashy stuff is nice from time to time, but I appreciate that I was able to give my wife the wedding of her dreams, my house was paid off before I even touched 30, and I'm able to provide a life for my daughter that I never had. I am eternally grateful," he said putting his head down, "I was there the day he died, and it still kills me that there was nothing I could've done to save him. It happened so fast."

"Yes, Sacario, Goldie spoke of you often. Between you, Jewel, and Brandon, you were all like his other sons. It's unfortunate that he's not here to see you today."

"We lost many of our people, but to me that motivates me more to continue on with G's mission with my brothers," he said taking a sip of the reddish orange liquid that filled his glass as he looked over at Hassan and Jewel.

"What about you, Mr. Williams?"

"Well, unlike Jewel and Sacario, I haven't been affiliated that long. I never got the chance to meet Mr. Smith, but I see the impact he had on Sacario and his brother-in-law Keith's lives. I actually went to college to be a director, but when I came back to the Bay Area, I didn't have any sort of direction. Now, I feel like God has aligned my opportunities because I'm sitting in front of you today."

"That's very important, sweetie," Laura said lighting a cigarette, "Diversification is key. You can definitely take a page from Golden's book. He had his hands in a little bit of everything. The more legit you seem, the less you appear on the radar. If a production studio is what you're after then I'm more than sure that can be accommodated. My brother Stevin and I are always looking for different business opportunities to put our money into. Speaking of, I just want to explain a few things before your trip tonight."

"Mom, I already filled them in," Jewel said taking a bite of the hot and flaky fish the server placed down on the table, "We're good."

"Tonight, you all will be taking a private jet to Moca, D.R. where you will meet Jewel's grandfather's right-hand man Luis Miguel. He then will escort you to Joseph Sr.'s estate in a village nearby."

"Is there anything we should be mindful of?" Sacario asked.

"I believe this trip serves a dual purpose. Jewel has been missing from our family for many years, so I think that his grandfather will be excited to have his only grandson in his presence, but do not confuse that with him not being focused on business as well. That comes first. You must prove your case as to why three works better than one. If you can do that then you all will become the sole suppliers to the M.A.C. Boy Empire along with many other operations across the United States and elsewhere. You could be given the opportunity to ensure that your families are more than take care of. I believe in my son, and he seems to feel very strongly about this arrangement, so I am going to trust his judgment. Here's to the success of this union," she said lifting her glass.

One-by-one, Jewel, Sacario, and Hassan all raised their glasses solidifying their pact.

"Well, if you boys are done eating, I can show you around the grounds," Laura offered.

"Count me in," Sacario said wiping his mouth before throwing his napkin down on the empty plate that sat in front of him.

"Jewel, can I talk to you?" Hassan asked finally working up the nerve.

"Uhhhhhh, yeah," he said standing up, "Ay, we'll catch up."

"Okay." Laura grabbed Sacario's hand and led him outside into the warm sunshine.

"What's up, man?"

"I know that when you called Sacario to come out here, you thought K was coming with him."

"Yeah, I mean, I'm a little disappointed that he's not here, but like I said, I respect his choice. He made it like a man, and how could I argue with him wanting to take care of my little sister and niece?"

"I want you to know that the vision Sacario has for the future of the M.A.C. Boys organization is the same one I have. I'm fully committed to this."

"I'm glad to hear it, but if Sacario vouches for you then that's good enough for me."

"Since we are now possibly going into this partnership together, I feel like I need to let you know something."

"And what's that?" Jewel asked completely oblivious.

"For the past couple of weeks, Diamond, and I have been seeing each other."

"Seeing each other how?"

"We've been on a few dates, and I have to admit that I really do care about her."

"My Diamond?" As much as she irritated him, he would always love her.

"Yes, and I mean no disrespect by this, but she is the sweetest, funniest, smartest, sexiest woman I know. If this deal really goes through then we will be working together, and I don't want to start off on a bad note, but at the same time, I feel like me and Diamond being together is something you need to know."

"Listen, Diamond is a grown woman, and I can't tell her who or who not to be with, but what I do have a say over is what happens around my son. I don't know how much of her past she has told you about, but the last guy she dealt with made her lose everything, and there was nothing I could really do about it. This time though, I won't be able to just sit back and watch her fall," Jewel said looking him in the eyes.

"If this was just a run, I wouldn't have even taken it to this point. I really care about, Diamond, so in no way am I trying to be her downfall."

Take her please, he thought. "All I care about is my son, bruh. Everything else is secondary to me. As long as you continue to keep that in mind, I don't think we'll have any problems."

"Like that?"

"Just like that."

"You have my word, man," he said standing up to shake Jewel's hand, "Now let's get this money."

$$$$$

Later That Night...

After spending the day getting to know Sacario and Hassan, Laura prepared for their trip. She had prepped Jewel as much as she could, but ultimately, the decision was up to his grandfather.

"Kurt, can you make sure the boys' bags are loaded in the car please?"

"Of course, Laurie," he said grabbing all of the luggage from the front door.

"Joe?" she screamed once he opened it.

"I'm sorry to just show up like this, but..."

"What are you doing here?"

"Is Jewel still here?" he asked looking around the front part of the house as he poked his head inside.

"Yes, but we're on our way out. You're too late, Joe. I know that you have gone out of your way to poison my son against me but no more. Jewel and I..."

"Laura, I came to talk to you. Can you give me five minutes please?"

"Dad?" Jewel asked coming downstairs, "What are you doing here?"

"I came to talk to your mother," he said never taking his eyes off her.

"Ummmm, okay, and you had to come all the way to Barbados to do that?"

"We can talk in my office, Joe," she said leading the way ready to get the conversation over with.

"Mom, the plane leaves in thirty minutes, so let's try and make this quick."

"Jewel, the plane leaves when I tell it to," she said shaking her head, "You have become so domestic, my love. You have so much to get used to again. Just give your father and I a few minutes, okay?"

Moments later, they arrived at the top level where Laura's office sat.

"You want anything to drink?" she asked fixing herself one.

"No, thank you. I don't drink anymore."

"Of course you don't," she said rolling her eyes, "So what do I owe this completely unexpected visit?"

"I know that for many years, things between us haven't always been great, but did it ever cross your mind to inform me that you were sending our son to see my father?"

"What could I do? That was at the request of Papi. I couldn't have stopped it even if I wanted to."

"A call would've been nice," he snapped.

"Joe, I don't owe you shit. For the last fifteen years, you have been nonexistent, but now we're co-parenting? Get the fuck out of here."

"Are you gonna hate me forever, Laura?" he asked hanging his head.

"Have you given me any reason not to?"

"I'm sorry."

"Why now?" she asked sitting down. She had waited over a decade to receive some sort of explanation from him.

"As kids, we were always so close. We did everything together, so when our fathers arranged for us to be married, it felt right. I got to marry the love of my life and my best friend, but the pressure our families put on me to be next on the throne became too much. I resented you because you seemed so comfortable in this world. Yeah, it was all we knew, but I knew there had to more to life."

"And where did that leave me, Joe?" Laura asked hiding her tears, "You never sat me down and said, 'Laura, I'm not in love with you anymore.' I didn't realize it until that slut wife of yours ended up pregnant."

"I just needed to run away from everything. I was tired of being my father's shadow. I wanted to be my own man and pave my own way."

"At the expense of your family?" Laura could never understand.

"I never said it was right."

"So what now? Why are you really here?"

"When I heard about Jewel going to D.R., it made me think. Since I have been married to Isabella, I haven't seen my family once. She convinced me that they were toxic to the new life we were creating. I sacrificed Papi because I wanted to appease her, but now with my only son going to see him, I feel like maybe it's time to finally go home."

"Your father asks about you every time I see him, and I hate that I never have anything new to say. He would love to see you. I know that for a fact. I was gonna go with Jewel, but if you're serious then maybe you should go with them."

"You know I never stopped loving you, right?" he said staring at her.

"It feels like you did," Laura said not trying to get wrapped up in the moment.

"I forgot about my best friend, and for that, I'm sorry," he said holding her hand. Laura felt her heart break all over again at the sight of his ring finger. Despite everything that had happened between them, deep down, she still loved him too.

Confused, Joe stood up and took her in his arms. Her familiar smell and the softness of her skin made him remember a time when he saw nothing but her. "I'm sorry," he said bending down to kiss her, and she couldn't help but to go back in time.

$$$$$

"Damn, they've been in there a long time," Jewel said looking down at his watch, "They gon' fuck around and make us have to fly out in the morning."

"You think they fucking, blood?" Sacario asked laughing.

"Man, come on," he said shaking his head.

"I'm just saying."

"Let me see what's taking so long," he said flying up the stairs.

"Change of plans, J," Joe said coming down with Laura following closely behind before Jewel reached the top.

"And what's that?"

"Your mother is going to stay here, and I'll be going to D.R. with you guys."

"Okay, but why the change of heart, Mom?"

"I think this is something that the Sanchez men need to do together. I'll be fine here. I was thinking about going into town and doing some shopping anyway."

"You sure about this?"

"I am more than sure. You will be going to your father's homeland. Who else better to go with?" she asked kissing him on the forehead, "If you guys want to make the time we scheduled then you better get a move on."

"Nice to meet you, Laura," Sacario said walking outside, "Thank you."

"Yes, thanks for having us," Hassan said walking out next.

"No problem, boys. Have a safe trip."

"So, you sure you don't wanna go?" Jewel asked again. He had to admit that he enjoyed spending time with her the past few weeks.

"Yes, baby," she laughed, "I know that you're adamant about going home after the trip with your grandfather, but it got me thinking."

"About?"

"About getting a place out in California. I wanna be able to see my grandkids more often. That 'Grandma Izzy' bullshit ain't gon' fly with me."

"Here you go."

"I'm serious, Jewel."

"Well, I can't speak for Isabella, but I would love to have you closer. We've already been apart for too long. I don't want any more time to go by."

"It's set then," she said trying to hold in her tears again.

"I love you," he said pulling her small frame closer to him, "Thank you for everything."

"Jewel, come on, son. We gotta go," Joe said walking back inside.

"I'll call you as soon as I get back to Sac," he said kissing Laura on the cheek before he walked out the door.

"Are you going to be here for a while?" Joe asked leaning against the oversized doorframe.

"Maybe, why?"

"I was hoping that we could continue our conversation after I get back."

"Call me. I might be here," she smiled before closing the door in his face.

"Ready, Pops?" Jewel asked throwing the last bag in the trunk.

"Yeah, but, hey, let me talk to you real quick," he said pulling him aside.

"What's up?"

"I told you that Reagan stopped by, right?"

"Yeah."

"She was really shaken up, Jewel. I wish I had more time to talk to her, but Gabrielle went into labor."

"Yeah, Sacario told me she had the baby."

"She is beautiful. She looks just like Gabrielle, but after Navaeh was born, all I could think about was you. Kiko and Isabella are there with Gabby now, so I don't feel so guilty about leaving, but it was important for me to talk to you before you got on that plane. With everything considered, are you sure that you're making the right decision?"

"I've never been surer about anything in my life. I tried to live that square life, but I was miserable every single day. I know that getting out of the game was easy for you and K-2..."

"It wasn't easy, Jewel. It was necessary."

"Nevertheless, it's not the life for me. I feel like all of my problems came from me trying to fit into these molds people put me in, but this is me, and I'm not gonna apologize for it anymore."

"I will always support you. You know that, right?"

"Thanks, Pops."

"And plus, I think that it's time for me to start dealing with some demons of my own," he said opening up the door for Jewel before getting in as Laura crossed his mind.

$$\$\$\$\$\$$$

Thirty minutes later, Laura heard a knock on the door. She had given her staff the night off in celebration of Jewel's return home, so she was forced to answer it herself.

"Who is it?" she yelled as she approached the door with a small, black .22 tucked behind her back.

There's no way they came back that fast, she thought as she peeked through the silk draped glass, but she couldn't see anything out in the darkness.

"Who is it?" she yelled again. There was still no answer until she heard the sounds of a baby crying. She picked up her gun and aimed it straight ahead and she slowly opened the door.

"Reagan?"

"Uh, Laura, hi," she said unable to take her eyes off her gun that was now pointed at her head, "I'm sorry to show up like this." Chase fidgeted in her arms as he noticed his unfamiliar surroundings.

"What are you doing here? Does Jewel know you're back?" she hurried to ask.

"No, not really."

"Girl, come on in here," she said already frustrated with Reagan's dramatics as she pulled her inside.

"I was hoping to catch him before he left."

"Well, you just missed him, so, now, why are you really here?"

The question caught Reagan off guard. "I'm here for my marriage," she admitted, "I know that my actions may not show it, but I love Jewel..."

"Like I said, Reagan, if you loved him then you would let him be. He doesn't need..."

"With all due respect, Laura, you haven't been around for a very long time now. You have no idea what that man put himself through, put his family through, all for the sake of this organization. I had to sit on the sideline while his best friend tried to murder him. I sat on the sideline while he did six months in jail for something that had nothing to do with him, so excuse me if I don't want him to go through that again. I know that my dislike for this life may have made me come across as weak, but I will do anything to protect my family, and I mean anything."

"Looks like someone found their backbone, huh?"

"Excuse me?"

"Listen, Reagan, my need to look after my son stews from my own insecurity of not being there. Despite what you may like or not like, this is Jewel's reality. I need to know that you are going to be there for the long haul and not give up at the first sight of trouble."

"I made a mistake by leaving, Laura, but on my son," she said looking down at his head full of curls, "I want nothing more than for this family to work."

"What's keeping you from leaving again?"

"Nothing, everything in me is telling me to run, but then I think about what my life would be like if Jewel wasn't in it, and I can't imagine being without him. He has been there for me in times where maybe he should've been the one to run away, but he didn't. He stood right by me, so, now, it's my turn. Honestly, we've been through much worse than this..."

"Give him here."

"Huh?"

"Chase. Give him here," Laura said extending her arms ready to receive her newly found grandson, "I can't say that I understand your methods, but I see the fire you have for my son. It's important to keep fighting because once one of you stops, that's it." She couldn't help but to think about her and Joe. "Jewel left about a half-hour ago, but if you leave now, you might be able to catch him."

"But, I..."

"Don't worry. I'll have my driver take you," she said disappearing into the living room to grab her phone with Chase snuggled against her chest.

"Thank you, Laura, I don't even know what to say,"

"Just say that you're going to take care of my son," Reagan heard through the darkness, "Hello, Kurt..."

$$$$$

Kurt pulled up to the small private airport that sat along the beach. Laura's Phenom 100 sat idly by as the crew made sure the fuel was full, and the cabin was completely stocked before they began boarding.

"Yo, this is phat as fuck," Sacario said noticing the inside as he climbed up the four small steps.

"Forreal though, I don't think I'ma be able to catch a regular flight ever again," Hassan laughed as he entered the cabin.

"Good evening, I'll be your pilot tonight. It should take us about ninety minutes to get to Moca. Ms. Smith made sure that everything has been taken care of, so just sit back and enjoy the flight," he said tipping his hat.

"You okay, son?" Joe asked placing his hand on Jewel's shoulder as he led them to the stairs.

"Yeah, I'm good," he said becoming lost in the lights on the runway.

"Jewel, Jewel," he heard someone yell behind him before he made his way inside. He turned around and saw Reagan running toward them.

"Rea?" he asked walking back down the steps, "What are you doing here?"

"Your mom…told me…you…were here," she said out of breath, "I was trying to catch you…before you left."

Jewel smiled at Laura's efforts. "Where's Chase?"

"She said she would watch him until we come back."

"We?"

"Listen, I know that me leaving like I did hurt you, and I'm sorry, but when your mom brought up the deal with your grandfather, my mind went to you being snatched away from me and the kids again."

"Reagan…"

"Jewel, let me finish. I have loved you since I met you, and although we've had our ups and downs, you were always there to support me. You always believed that we were gonna make it, so now it's my turn to have the same faith," she said kissing him on the lips.

"What does that mean?"

"That we're married now. I don't know what our future holds, but I don't care as long as it involves us and our kids," she said handing him an envelope.

"What's this?"

"I went to the doctors when I was home," she said nervously.

"Is everything okay?" he asked hurrying to read the paper that sat inside, "You're pregnant?" He couldn't stop the smile from spreading across his face.

"Yep, ten weeks."

Jewel grabbed her around her waist and kissed her again. "I love you."

"I love you too, and I'm always gonna worry about you just like you worry about me. That's never gonna change, but I couldn't let you do this alone."

"You sure? There's no turning back after this, Rea," he said firmly holding onto her shoulders.

"I'm ready."

"Let's do this then." Jewel guided her onto the place like she was precious cargo.

"Reagan, what are you doing here?" Sacario asked getting up.

"I talked to Kiko, and she made me realize how stupid I was being," she admitted.

"My Kiko?"

"Yes," Reagan smiled.

"Well, I'm glad you came, sis."

"Me too," she said sitting down, "Hi, Hassan." She was surprised to see him after everything that happened. She just prayed that Diamond was far behind.

"Hey, Reagan."

After about an hour, everyone was asleep except Jewel. He looked down at Reagan sleeping on his shoulder, and he couldn't hide his excitement. For the first time, his family and career seemed to finally be coming together as one. As he stared ahead under the dimmed lighting, his phone vibrated in his pocket.

"I was thinking about you," he said answering.

"I can tell," Gabrielle said softly into the phone.

"How are you?"

"Good, figuring that I just pushed an eight-pound baby out of my chotch. When are you coming to see us?"

"As soon as I touch back down. I promise."

"I can't wait for you to see Naveah. She looks just like us."

"Yeah, Pops told me that she looked like you spit her out. I know K-2 is mad," Jewel said laughing a little.

"Speaking of Dad, have you talked to him?"

"Have you?" he asked not knowing what his story was.

"He came up to the hospital with Keith and Mom, and he stayed until after I had Naveah, but then he told my mom that he had to suddenly fly out for business. I don't know what's going on."

"Listen, you should talk to him…"

"Jewel, if you know something then say it," Gabrielle said trying not to wake K-2 and the baby.

"He's with me."

"Where, in Barbados?"

"My mom arranged for me to meet Abuelo."

"Papi?" she asked in disbelief, "Daddy hasn't talked to him in years."

"We're flying out to Moca tonight."

"For what? I understand that a family reunion is needed, but is this the right time?"

"I had nothing to do with this, Gabrielle. You're mad at the wrong person. When my mom said that Grandpa wanted to see me, I was fully prepared to go alone, but Pops showed up right before I left. I think he needs this."

"My mom is not gonna be happy," she said shaking her head.

"You can tell her to relax. Family is the most important thing we have, and this trip is about that reconnection," he said leaving out the true details behind it. He didn't want her worrying.

"Please be careful, Jewel," she said not fully convinced by her brother's reassuring words.

"Always."

"Well, it's late. Tell Dad that I'll be calling bright and early tomorrow, so he better have his ass up."

"I will."

"I love you, J."

"I love you too. I'll see you when I get home. Kiss Naveah for me."

"Good night."

An hour later, Jewel lifted his head realizing that they had reached their destination.

"Mr. Sanchez, welcome to Moca," the captain said opening the cabin doors. Jewel was amazed by all of the lights. The city was beautiful.

"Wow," was all Joe could say as he helped Reagan off of the plane. The crisp air sent chills through him. He was looking at his home with new eyes.

"Ms. Smith arranged to have a car escort you to your destination," the captain said, "It should be up there to your right."

"Thanks, man," Sacario said grabbing his bags.

"What now?" Reagan asked trying to wake up as she surveyed the scenery.

"I guess we're about to find out," Jewel said walking up to the car that awaited them.

Knock. Knock. Knock. Knock. He lightly tapped on the glass.

"Señor Sanchez?" a young guy asked as he rolled down the window.

"Uh, yeah, that's me."

"Mi nombre es Tomás. Papi me envió a recoger usted y sus invitados," he smiled, "Bienvenida."

"What?" Jewel never learned to speak Spanish at no fault of his own.

"Son, he said his name is Tomás, and Papi sent him to pick us up."

"Oh, okay, cool. I'm Jewel, this is my wife Reagan, and my business partners Sacario and Hassan."

Tomás just continued to smile. English wasn't his strong suit.

"Me disculpo, Tomás. Jewel no habla español pero él dijo que esta es su esposa de Reagan, y sus socios de negocios Sacario y Hassan."

"Very nice to meet you," he struggled to say, "This way."

He grabbed their bags and loaded them into the trunk. Once everyone was inside the car, Tomás began his tour around Moca.

"Yo, it seems cool out here. There's way more people than I thought," Jewel admitted as he watched the night life that filled the streets.

"Just wait and see." Joe sat back with a smirk on his face.

Mile after mile, Jewel noticed civilization disappearing. Tomás had driven so far out of the city that they were soon surrounded by nothing but acres and acres of luscious green land. The dark umbrella of trees above them hid their path in the darkness until they stopped in front of a river.

"What the fuck is this?" he asked uncomfortable with his unfamiliar surroundings.

"Tendrá que tomar el barco amarrado al árbol de la aldea," Tomás said speaking to Joe, "Luis Miguel se encontrará con usted en el otro lado."

"What he say?" Jewel asked ready for an explanation.

"He said get in the boat," Joe laughed.

"What?"

"You see that village over there?" He pointed across the cool water to the other side.

"Yeah."

"Well, that's where we're going, and this is the only way to get there. You can't drive a car through water, Jewel."

"I don't know how to drive a boat. There's not even a motor on it."

"Get in, pretty boy. I got this," he said rolling up his sleeves.

"Ok, Rambo," Jewel said helping Reagan onto the boat first. Sacario and Hassan were completely out of their element, so they remained quiet.

"I used to boat across these waters all the time," Joe said reminiscing, "Believe it or not, this is where I lived until I was 14."

"That's crazy." Jewel couldn't imagine his father coming from such a remote place.

"Gracias, Tomás," he said handing him a $50 bill, "Me lo llevo de aquí."

"Welcome home, Junior," Tomás said getting back into the car. He didn't wait long before he headed back to the city.

"Jewel, I don't know about this," Reagan said standing up on the rickety boat. The back and forth sensation made her sick to her stomach.

"Pops, are you sure you got this?"

"Yeah, son," he said untying the boat from the tree it was attached to, "Ya'll ready?"

No one said a word.

Joe picked up the two small oars that sat alongside the boat and started rowing into the night. He couldn't see where he was going, but something was guiding him to their destination through the quiet waters. Forty-five minutes later, he found himself approaching the river bank as he saw the sun on the horizon.

"Now what?" Jewel asked helping Reagan onto dry land.

"Hola, Junior," an older man in all grey suit said as he walked toward them.

"Luis?" Joes asked. He dropped the rope that he was wrapping around a small tree and ran to him unable to keep his tears from falling. Everyone remained quiet while their embrace continued. "Son, I want you to meet your grandfather's right hand Luis Miguel. He's like my second father."

"Nice to meet you, sir," he said honored.

"You too. This day has been a long time coming. Vamos. Papi awaits," Luis said as he led them up a hill to a small village. Huts covered in multi-colored metal siding sat side-by-side, and chickens and goats roamed freely as the people slept.

"Abuelo really lives here?" Jewel asked in disbelief as he continued behind Joe.

"Believe it or not, yes. This is where I grew up, where he grew up, and his father before him. This village has been home to our family for many generations, but even after Papi started making enough money to leave, he never did."

"Well, why didn't he use some of that money to fix it up or something?"

"He loves its simplicity."

"Jewel, Junior, you two come with me. I'll have Maria show your wife and friends to their rooms."

"I thought the meeting included all of us?"

"It does, but this is not that," Luis said walking into the modest two-story house that sat all the way in the back of the village.

"Rea, you good?"

"Yeah, I'll be fine. I'm tired anyway. I'll just go lay down."

"Okay, see you in a little bit."

"Maria, llevarlos a sus habitaciones y hacer que lo que necesitan."

"Si, señor," the young house servant said as she grabbed Reagan's bags.

"She will take care of you all," Luis assured her.

"In a minute, blood," Sacario said following behind Reagan and Hassan.

"You guys ready?"

"Yep," Jewel said feeling his heart beat out of his chest.

Even though he knew Papi was his grandfather that didn't settle his nerves any. There was still a lot at stake.

Knock. Knock. Knock. Knock.

"Come in," they heard a raspy voice say from behind the door.

"Papi, Junior and Jewel have arrived," Luis said walking into his study.

Jewel saw the shadow of his grandfather as he ashed his cigar in in a glass tray that sat on his desk before he walked around to face them.

"It's been a long time, son," Papi said standing in front of Joe.

"It has," he said noticing his hair. It was much whiter than he was used to.

"When Laura informed me that you would be taking her place in this trip, I thought she was playing some cruel joke on me, but here you stand."

"I'm sorry for letting so much time go by."

"It's all in the past now, mijo. We are now building our future."

"I would like that," he said wrapping his arms around his father. The comforting smell of stale cigar smoke and freshly roasted coffee soothed him.

"And this must be Jewel," he said smiling.

"Nice to meet you, sir," he said trying not to stare, but he couldn't help but notice how much they looked alike.

"Sir? I'm your Abuelo, Jewel. No reason to be so formal," he said giving him a hug, "I hate that it took so long for us to finally meet, but I am a firm believer that everything happens for a reason. Although you never knew about me, I definitely knew about you. Your mother made sure of that. She has kept me up-to-date on all of your progress over the years. While there were some moments where I was extremely proud of you, I do also know that you dropped the ball on many occasions as well."

"I..."

"Please, no explanation needed, Jewel. A lot of it was no fault of your own. Your father must also take some responsibility."

"Papi, I...," Joe said lowering his head.

"Joe, I respect your wanting to leave the life. I just don't respect how you did. You left your family to fend for themselves, and as a result, that's exactly what they did."

"I know I should've been there, but I can't keep beating myself up about the past. I'm standing here now with my son," he said placing his arm around Jewel's shoulder, "And I don't plan on leaving ever again."

"Before we start, Joe, I need to know that you are not going to be an interference of any kind. Your separation is your own. Jewel has a job to do."

"That's why I'm here."

Joe's response was like music to his ears. He missed his son, but he couldn't excuse the life he lived. After his divorce with Laura, Papi saw him as weak.

"As a 76-year old man, I don't have the energy anymore. I forgive you, hijo," he said kissing him on both cheeks. He was now ready to walk into the future with his bloodline by his side. He wrapped his arms around Joe and Jewel's shoulders before bowing his head into the early morning light.

"Here's to new beginnings," he said proudly.

$$$$$

"Man, I feel like we're on *Survivor* or some shit," Hassan said unpacking.

"I don't think Jewel knew it was gonna be all this, but whatever we have to do, I'm willing to do. A little water ain't never hurt anybody."

"Says the nigga who can't swim," Hassan laughed.

"Once we finish up here, everything can go back to normal, and then you can run your ass back to Diamond."

"Don't play me, blood. We've only been kicking it for a few weeks."

"Did you ever talk to Jewel?"

"Yep."

"What he say?"

"That's for me to know and you not to. I'm here, right? We're good."

"Alright, I can respect that," Sacario said wanting to be sensitive to his friend's privacy.

"I can't front, we made it official before I left, but to have Jewel's blessing means a lot. I'm not tryna start this shit out on the wrong foot..."

Reagan stood against the wall continuing to listen to Hassan and Sacario's conversation. In search of the bathroom led her right to their room, and she couldn't resist. Overhearing Diamond's name got her thinking. They hadn't talked since Gabrielle's baby shower, but obviously, they had a lot to catch up on. She walked back to her room, but when she saw that Jewel still hadn't returned yet, she closed the door, grabbed her phone, and laid down across the bed.

"Hello?" Diamond asked with sleep in her voice.

"Hey."

"Rea? What time is it? Is everything okay?"

"Yeah, everything is fine. I just saw Hassan."

"Okay?" she said feeling her heart drop down to her stomach.

"He seems like he really likes you."

"Listen, Reagan, I know that this entire situation was messy, but I just want you to know that I never..."

"I'm happy for you. He's really a good guy," she said wanting to leave the past where it belonged.

"He is," Diamond said before getting quiet again. The dead air on the line suffocated the both of them. After a few more silent moments, neither one could take it anymore.

"I'm sorry," they said at the same time.

"Why are you sorry?" Diamond asked, "I was the asshole in this situation."

"Yeah, you were, but this is partially my fault too. I guess that deep down, I knew that you still had feelings for Jewel, but in a way, I enjoyed rubbing it in your face that we were together. It was petty."

"Jewel will always mean a lot to me, but I held on for so long because I didn't want to believe that he didn't love me anymore. He always talked about his parents' situation, and it felt like he was doing the same thing to me. Now is different though. I want you and Jewel to know that I'm really serious about Hassan. He makes me feel like myself again, and I would hate it if people tried to act like he's just some rebound."

"At the end of the day, our sons are brothers, and with this baby, it solidifies that."

"Baby? You're pregnant?"

"Yeah, two months."

"Congratulations," Diamond said still having mixed feelings.

"I don't want us to have bad blood, you know?"

"I don't either."

"Hassan spoke to Jewel about you. I think it went okay being that I didn't have to pull Jewel off him. I realized that we're all connected, and I don't start hating you again. I forgive you."

"Really?"

"It's not like we're gonna be going on double-dates anytime soon, but I do wanna start over."

"I would like that."

"I know it's early, but I had to let you know that I'm rooting for you and Hassan. You deserve to finally be free, Diamond."

"I appreciate you, Rea. That really means a lot. See you when you get back," she said hanging up.

Reagan hated being the bigger person sometimes, but with her future full of so many new possibilities, she had no room for hate. As she continued to wait for Jewel, she closed her eyes but drifted off to sleep before he ever made it back.

Sasha Ravae

$$$$$

Later That Day…

"He's ready for you," Luis said opening the door to Papi's study where he and Joe were both waiting. Hassan and Sacario walked into the small room first, but Jewel stayed back needing to talk to Reagan before he went in.

"You okay?" she asked smoothing out his dark blue jacket.

"Yeah, me and Pops were up all morning talking to my grandfather. The deal is basically set."

"I know. When I woke up you still weren't there."

"I'm sorry I'm putting you through all this again, Rea, especially now," he said softly rubbing her belly.

"When I got home, Sacario's wife Kiko was there, and we spent the whole night talking. It was different, you know? She's in the same situation we are. She's been through it all with Sacario, and because of that, she made me realize that my place is right by your side. Who else I'ma ride for?"

"You have no idea how much I need you, Reagan," he said pulling her to him.

"I may not agree with what you do a hundred-percent of the time, but I've been committed to you even before the ring. If you're in, I'm in," she said kissing him.

"Jewel," Joe said coming out, "You ready, son?"

"Yeah," he said turning around, "Here I come. Give me two seconds."

"Go, babe." She was finally at peace.

"They can wait," he said kissing her back, "When we get back home, we're gonna get back to us. This pregnancy won't be like the last time. I promise you that. I am honored to be learning from my grandfather and getting closer to my mom and pops in the process, but you, this baby, and the boys are still my first priority. This is just for fun," he smiled.

"Well, you better get in there," she said pushing him toward the door.

Jewel took a breath and one last look at Reagan before he walked in.

"Nieto," Papi said standing up, "Nice for you to join us."

"Sorry, Abuelo," Jewel said standing beside Hassan and Sacario who were both lined up in front of his desk.

"If you are now ready, we can get started," he said breathing out a thick cloud of smoke.

"Yes, sir."

"I know that Laura has already explained to you the situation at hand, so I will not waste anymore of our time. With Laura and Stevin no longer in the role of distribution, I need to be reassured that one, Jewel, you are ready for this, and two, that your friends here are in a position to support you."

"Abuelo, since I was 15-years old, Golden had been a very strong influence in my life. I love my dad, I do, but Golden is the reason I am the man I am today. I understand that the responsibilities of my mother and uncle far exceeds those of just being on the corner, but the goal still remains the same—to ensure that our families are in a position to succeed and to continue to be prosperous. The loyalty I have for my brothers is based on the same thing, and that is why they are standing beside me today."

"That's all I needed to hear, Jewel. Family is what this whole thing has been about, and you can see when you don't have that, you have nada," Papi said looking over at Joe who was standing right beside him, "With my son and grandson now back home, I am more than sure that Jesus Christo has ordained this himself. I am ready to get started."

"Thank you, Mr. Sanchez, sir," Sacario said stepping forward, "We will not let you down."

Maria walked into the office with a tray full of rum shots, and one-by-one, each man took a glass waiting for Papi to continue speaking.

"I appreciate you all being here and dedicating yourself to the cause," he said raising his glass, "To my son, to my grandson, and to the preservation of the Sanchez-Smith cartel. Here's to the future."

The End

BLACK EDEN PUBLICATIONS

CPSIA information can be obtained
at www.ICGtesting.com
Printed in the USA
LVOW04s1329091215

465959LV00038B/1278/P

9 781511 836081